GANGSTER DREAMS

A Novel

By

DARRIEN HALL

Milligan Books   California

Published by:

Milligan Books
1425 W. Manchester Ave., Suite C
Los Angeles, CA 90047
(323)750-3592
http://www.milliganbooks.com

Formatted by Black Butterfly Press

First Printing: June 2001

10 9 8 7 6 5 4 3 2 1

ISBN   1-881524-97-3

Milligan Books
1425 W. Manchester Ave., Suite C
Los Angeles, CA 90047
(323)750-3592
http://www.milliganbooks.com

Printed in the United States of America

Dedication

This book is dedicated to my father, Robert Hall, brother Jerry Davis, best friend Darryl Carr, Aurelius Bailey, my brother-in-law, Ray Ray Browning, a true gangster, my family and friends, who believed in me, and especially my mother Vera Bernice Hall, who has loved me unconditionally and has guided me and supported me.

Much Love,

Pasadena in the House

About the Author

Darrien Hall, a 36-year old Los Angeles native, is the father of six children. Mr. Hall has five sisters and six brothers. He has aspired to be a writer for many years. He enjoyed baseball in high school and was a star pitcher. His hobbies are bowling and fishing.

Mr. Hall wants to send a message to young people who glorify the fast life. As the pages turn, traveling the fast-lane journey, the reader will get a glimpse of the flip side of what appears to be a good life.

Darrien Hall's cautionary tale sends a loud and compelling message to the young: Don't use or sell drugs and stay in school.

Darrien Hall

Darrien Hall

Marquis　　Audonnis　　Aurelius　　Aujulius　　Corey

Chapter I

"Deangelo, what are you still doing up? It's two in the morning. You gotta go to school tomorrow, boy."

Deangelo looked up to see his mother standing in a triangle of light outside his bedroom door. From where she stood, with her hands on her hips, he could see his mother's frown. He hadn't meant to wake her. He just hadn't heard her slip open his bedroom door, he was so engrossed in watching *Scarface*.

"Aw, Mom, just let me hear this line one more time....Please."

With a pleading look in his eyes, Deangelo turned back to the TV. It wasn't too late. Here was his favorite line.

"I'm the bad guy. It takes people like me so you can point your fingers and say that's the bad guy," the gangster barked. *"People like you don't have the balls to be like me."*

Trance-like, Deangelo silently mouthed each word along with the actor since he had memorized most of the lines in the film.

His mother's voice snatched him back to reality.

"Deangelo, turn that mess off. I'm really getting worried about you with these gangster movies. You know I raised you to be a Christian." His mother's eyes narrowed into pinpoints of concern. "I don't like you watching mess like this. This is as bad as that Rap music."

Deangelo looked up from the TV screen and to placate his mother, gave her his winning smile.

"Mom, this has nothing to do with being a Christian. Sometimes, wouldn't you like to have some nice things?"

"Deangelo, as long as I got my health and strength, I don't worry about material things."

"But I'd like to give them to you. Mom, there's so much I want for you."

2

"I know, son. You just get to bed so you can get a good education and give it to yourself." His mother walked over and hugged Deangelo. "Now go to bed. You're getting to be as tall as me."

Deangelo reached out and hugged his mother back. He wished he could buy her another terry cloth robe. The faded pink one she'd been wearing for years was nearly threadbare. "Good night, Mom."

He got up and cut the TV off. As soon as he heard her houseshoes scraping the floor down the hall, he began snoring. After he heard his mother close the door to her bedroom, he tiptoed back to the TV and cut it on. He used a pair of pliers to turn down the volume and once again focused on the small black and white television set with a hanger for an antenna.

Within minutes he heard his mother snoring again. Deangelo relaxed. He lay on his bed, arms folded behind his head. Wide-eyed, his line of vision was glued to his broken down TV. He was still mesmerized, as he watched his favorite movie, *Scarface*. This was a regular routine for him. He'd never disobeyed his mother...that is, until now.

At fifteen, Deangelo was fascinated with these kinds of gangster films. He was totally immersed as the movie unveiled its drama, showing how this poor immigrant, who was no one special, rose to power on the streets. It was the kind of power Deangelo felt he could only dream about. A kind of power he secretly craved. Power which thrilled and excited Deangelo's imagination every time he would let his mind run with these spellbinding sagas.

This man came from nothing, had nothing, and was now on top with everything, or so it seemed. The world appeared to be literally at his feet. His cunning and ruthlessness afforded him all that he thought he wanted and more. People respected him wherever he went, no matter what the situation, even if it was out of fear. No one dared cross him, and if they did, he saw to it that it usually cost them their lives; it was all part of how you played the game.

The violence and death involved were not especially appealing to Deangelo as his mother had tried her best to instill in him a solid Christian belief system. Nevertheless, he felt it came with the territory. You just had to do what you had to do. It was the price you had to pay in order to play. It would somehow, in the long run, be worth it to get what you wanted, to be able to have something of your own, to be respected, to be one of the major players in the gangster world. To be able to wheel and deal with the big boys.

Deangelo was desperate for a change in his life. As a poor Black boy, he felt that becoming a gangster was the only way he would be able to really have anything in his life. He was constantly embarrassed and shamed by the poverty and kind of life that seemed to consume him on a daily basis.

There never seemed to be enough money to go around. His family always had to make do, or settle for less, it seemed. They moved constantly, or the landlord was threatening to kick them out.

But this time, somehow, they were managing to hold on to things for the past year.

His mother always said it was by the grace of God. Because God loved them, He would provide for them. But where was God now, when they needed Him? It didn't seem fair. Why couldn't his family live in a nice new home, wear expensive clothing and drive a big fancy car like other people he saw? Most of all, why couldn't they have plenty of money? Or at least be able to comfortably make ends meet without always having so many problems, problems that were always about not enough money.

Deangelo would never forget the day he came home from school, just in time to hear his mother pleading with the owner Mr. Carpenter for more time to pay the rent. They were two months behind and had made payment arrangements. His father was supposed to have given his mother the money two days earlier.

"I'm sorry, Mrs. Jackson. But if you can't make a payment of at least one hundred dollars, you'll have to be out by the end of the week."

Mr. Carpenter's face looked sorry, but he still was adamant about wanting his money.

Deangelo could tell by the crumpled look on his mother's face that it hurt her to be unable to pay this man.

"Mr. Carpenter, I know I said I'd have the money today, but please. Just give me a few more days..."

He could see how embarrassed she was and how desperately she was begging for more time. It seemed to be taking its toll on her, and this really bothered him.

His mother was beginning to develop deep furrows around her eyes and her mouth. He remembered how young and pretty his mother used to look. Now she was beginning to look old before her time.

Anyhow, where was his father, Shorty? Why was he always leaving them in a jam like this?

One hundred dollars, a measly hundred bucks! Deangelo remembered seeing how one gangster from the movies he loved so much lit his cigar with hundred dollar bills like it was nothing. He couldn't help but think how, to the gangster, one hundred dollars was expendable. Unfortunately, here in his family's situation, one hundred dollars might as well have been one million. They simply didn't have it.

A simple hundred dollars would make the difference in them keeping their shelter and saving his mother from this kind of constant stress and humiliation. Deangelo knew that money would make a big difference in most of the choices he found himself having to make in his young life. He was tired of always having to make excuses. But where was he going to get one hundred dollars?

Once again he wondered where the hell was Shorty? What could he possibly do? If only there was some way he could help. He felt so weak, helpless, and frustrated because he wanted desperately to help his mom.

Fortunately, just as Deangelo walked onto the porch, like an answer to one of his mother's prayers, his father pulled up. This time, the family hadn't seen Shorty for the last five days.

He sauntered up on the porch, argued with the landlord, and complained about things that were wrong with the house. Finally, reluctantly, he reached into his pocket and made the payment, putting a temporary end to the crisis.

With no apology, Shorty went into the house and took a shower. When he came out of the bathroom, he spent a few minutes playfully hugging Deangelo's mom.

"Get away from me, Shorty," Bernice said, shaking her head. At the same time, relief had relaxed the worry lines in her face—for now.

Shorty grabbed a piece of fried chicken Bernice had cooked. After saying a few words to console Deangelo, he took off again, for how long, no one knew.

Deangelo's family consisted of two parents. But his father, Shorty, who was a hustler and gambler, was rarely home. Shorty spent most of his time at the gambling shacks he ran, but somehow he never seemed to come out on top. He was known to be a player and often squandered his money on women and fast living, instead of taking care of his home and family, and most of all just being there for them.

He loved them, but somehow didn't seem to understand the value or necessity of a total commitment to his clan. He didn't seem to understand the value of his presence in the home. It was as if he had one foot in both worlds and wasn't winning in either one. He was always looking for that big win, which never came.

The wear from constantly running the streets and staying up all night was finally beginning to catch up with him. He had a nagging cough and didn't seem to be himself.

Deangelo's mother, Bernice, was a hard-working, Christian, church-going woman. She did the best she could with what she had. It seemed like she was always working either at home, church, or sewing for extra money. It was she who provided most of the love and support for her family.

She labored relentlessly to provide for her children and keep them out of trouble. She was constantly on Deangelo and Doris about going to school and getting an education so they could improve themselves.

Bernice especially wanted to shield her son from the kind of lifestyle in which her husband and older son had found themselves so enmeshed. She was always talking about the kind of friends Deangelo should hang around with and the places she approved of him going, as well as the things he should be doing with his free time.

"Idle hands are the Devil's workshop," she would always say. She told Deangelo that she couldn't bear to see him behind bars like Penthouse and only wanted the best for him. She talked about how she was counting on him to make it.

His sister, Doris, was twenty-five, with two boys, ages five and three. Doris was also into the church and did her best to be a good mother and help out at home, although her county check would only go so far. Doris adored Deangelo. They had a very loving sibling relationship, and Deangelo spent a lot of time with her boys.

There was also his older brother, Ajulius, known as "Penthouse." He was serving eighteen years in prison for murder, as his violent nature had finally caught up with him. Ajulius had a ruthless reputation on the streets and was feared by everyone.

Penthouse was locked up during most of Deangelo's life and was definitely not able to provide his younger brother with a positive role model image. For some reason, he always acted as though he resented Deangelo, and would never spend time with him when he was home. However, whenever he made phone calls home, he always talked to his younger brother about staying out of trouble and not getting involved in the game.

And finally, there was his sister's husband, Chris, who did act as somewhat of a mentor to the teenager, but was also in prison for grand-theft auto, serving three to five years for a crime he didn't commit. He was basically a good father and gave Deangelo all the attention that time would allow, but his sense of loyalty was a bit misplaced. Chris chose to be locked up instead of telling the truth about what really happened. There was no way he was snitching on his best friend. This was a choice, he later grew to regret.

Deangelo loved and cherished his mother, and cared very deeply for all his family. During his younger years, he spent much of his time in church and at the Boy's Club, a place he enjoyed going, which pleased his mother very much. She felt that he would be safe and out of trouble as long as he was there. He always tried his best to do whatever he could to stay out of trouble and be supportive. He helped out at home whenever he could, despite the situation.

The family rented a rundown, but clean, three-bedroom house located in the lower income part of Pasadena. Their living quarters were as well kept as his mother could manage.

Even so, Deangelo was growing tired of hand-me-down clothes, lunch tickets at school, eviction notices, and excuses for not having and being unable to do the simple things he desired. His neat, but sparsely furnished, bedroom, which was really a very large service porch that had been converted, seemed to close in on him when his concentration was broken by his mother calling.

"Deangelo, Deangelo! Boy you'd better turn off the TV set right this minute and go to sleep! Right this minute young man. Do you know what time it is? You have school in the morning. Don't make me have to come in there now." His mother's voice traveled down the hallway.

"Okay, Ma. I'm turning it off....For real this time." Deangelo called out as he stuffed a towel at the bedroom door to make it appear that the lights had been turned off.

Deangelo pondered his situation. It didn't seem fair. Why should some people have everything, while others had nothing? From what Deangelo gathered, there were two kind of people in life; the hustlers and the workers. The hustlers never worked, and the workers never hustled. It seemed like the hustlers had all the money.

He had watched his parents work hard all his life and so far had seen that they were just barely able to make ends meet. Sometimes, he even went along to help with the janitorial service they were struggling to get off the ground. This was mainly because his father had not shown up for work and had usually not been seen for two or three days.

Deangelo often wondered if this was what life was all about. Why couldn't things be different for them? Do you just work hard, struggling everyday, only to still end up with nothing to show for it but bills? Is this what God wanted for them, was this his plan; or do you have to just go out there and take what you want like the gangsters did it?

It sure didn't seem to him, that a person would ever be able to accomplish anything working a nine-to-five. He longed to see his mother with a nice house, and a new car, and fine clothes to wear. He especially wanted her not to have to worry about a roof over their heads and the basic necessities of living.

The lavish lifestyles and excitement of the gangster's world appeared to be so far out of reach, sometimes it seemed like a mirage. But it definitely looked like a way out.

Through the rest of the movie, Deangelo attentively hung on to every word Scarface uttered.

"The world is mine!"

"You have to take what you want; you can't trust anyone!"

The scenes were permanently embedded in his brain. He fantasized about being in that role himself. Envisioning himself as the boss. Imagining he was calling all the shots, making all the big deals, being chauffeur-driven, and dining and dancing in all the finest places.

When the movie ended, Deangelo reluctantly turned off the TV, thinking long and hard about what he had just seen. This was the kind of life he wanted: money, power, women, and respect. He did an imitation of Scarface.

"To get women, first get money! People like you don't have the balls to be like me. I got the balls," he muttered, drifting off to sleep.

Time flew by so quickly that Deangelo felt like he had just laid his head down, when three hours later his mother awakened him.

"Get up, boy, and don't you give me no excuses!" His mother stood over his twin bed.

"I'm up." Deangelo turned back over and put the pillow over his head. He was so sleepy.

"Deangelo, wake up, you hear me, boy? Get out of that bed right now, young man!" His mother pulled the covers from over his head.

"I've told you, time and time again, about staying up all night with that TV. I'm gonna take that thing out of your room if you can't be more responsible."

"I said I'm up, Mom."

"You know that as long as you live in this house, you have to go to school to get your education, so that you can make something of yourself."

Reluctantly, Deangelo rolled out of bed. Half-awake, groaning, and tired, he began his morning rituals. His mother made sure he went into the bathroom before she went and started breakfast. Since he was the first one up, he didn't have to wait for the bathroom. No matter what he really wore, every morning he pretended he was getting dressed up like the gangsters he secretly emulated.

He imagined putting on an expensive Armani suit, a shiny, new pair of alligator shoes, a new, creased Stetson hat, a Rolex watch, and extravagant jewelry, like big diamond rings and gold pins. He saw himself getting ready to go out to handle his business because he was the top dog. He was number one.

"This world is mine!" He mimicked in the mirror.

However, no matter how much he pretended, he kept his make-believe world hidden inside himself. No one knew what he was doing, or why it took him so long every morning in the bathroom. No one knew what he secretly longed for either. Surely, no one understood the deep impressions that were being imprinted on his young mind.

Once he finally arrived at school, Deangelo usually enjoyed his classes. He was a good student, a fast learner, and usually made good grades in his classes. The only time he would shut down was when he encountered problems with his white teachers. Most of the time, he didn't feel comfortable with them.

Despite his occasional attitude, both his Black and White teachers talked about what potential he had, and constantly told him that he was capable of making something of himself. Unfortunately, he did not see this as a way out

17

of his situation. He wasn't aware of anything in school that would get him the kind of money, excitement, and respect that being on top in the gangster life would provide.

Because of this, he saw school as a cosmic joke. Go get an education so you could die broke. No, he wanted fast money. However, at the moment, school gave him a temporary escape from his depressing reality.

Here he didn't have the constant reminders of his impoverished lifestyle. Most times things seemed to be all right, almost everything, or at least, most things were equal.

Except for when he needed money for extracurricular activities or special events, and there was none. Frequently, even lunch money was a problem. The majority of the days that this became a problem, he was bailed out by one of the many females at school, who were trying their best to get something going with him. For some reason, he didn't understand why they seemed to be drawn to him. Then, he was all too painfully reminded of his financial status, which both hurt and angered him, although he did an excellent job suppressing his true feelings.

When this would happen, he would make up some convenient excuse for not being able to attend or participate, but he would never let on that *lack of money* was the real culprit. Because of this, he was also basically quiet and kept to himself most of the time, although he seemed to be able to get along quite well with almost everyone, as he was a kindhearted person, with a very likeable personality.

The girls really liked him and were always doing things to let him know they were interested. There where occasions when some of his female classmates almost came to blows for the opportunity to date him. He seemed to take this unsolicited attention in stride because he had yet to meet anyone who really got next to him.

Deangelo had one best friend named Buck. The two of them were inseparable at school and everywhere else. His mother, however, did not approve of Buck.

"That boy is nothing but trouble," Bernice preached at Deangelo whenever his friend was mentioned. Nevertheless, he was closer to Buck than he was to his own brother, Penthouse, who he really did not know very well. Deangelo and

Buck walked to the bus stop together every morning and went to the same classes together. Buck, who was also fifteen, lived two doors down from Deangelo. He had a reputation of being a bully. He was large for his age and slightly muscular. He had a volatile temper, and most of the students, as well as some of the teachers, feared him. Buck had spent time in juvenile hall for selling drugs.

Rumor had it that he carried a gun to school everyday and was not afraid to use it. At first, Deangelo never really believed this, because he had never seen that side of Buck, nor had he ever seen him with a gun.

That is, until one day, when the two boys were riding home on the bus, they and a few friends began bagging on each other. This was their usual pastime, where they played the dozens and tried verbal one-upmanship on each other.

Buck made a comment about a boy named Tion's girlfriend. "That bitch is so ugly, she has to sneak up on a glass of water," he said, roaring in sidesplitting laughter." At least I have a woman. The only person you can go out with is your mama," Tion joked, causing everyone on the bus to laugh so hard that they were almost in tears.

Suddenly Buck grew quiet. He said nothing else the entire bus ride home. When the bus reached their stop, the boys got off and began walking home.

Without warning, Buck grabbed Tion by his throat, shoving the end of a .38 in his mouth.

"Nigga, you ever talk about my mama again and I'll blow your fuckin' head off," Buck threatened through clinched teeth. His face curled into hatred. Buck's eyes pierced Tion's like two daggers.

"I'm sorry, Buck. We cool. Man, I'm sorry." Tears streamed down Tion's olive-toned face. He held his body tensed as Buck collared him with his left hand and held the gun with the right.

What seemed like hours passed, however it was only a few minutes.

"Man, be cool," Deangelo said softly.

Slowly, Buck relaxed his grip on Tion.

Deangelo gave a sigh of relief when Buck eventually let Tion run home, scared half to death. Deangelo and Buck continued to walk home, never mentioning the incident between them again. That was when Deangelo realized that the rumors about Buck and his gun were true.

Buck was not really into school and often had difficulties. Although he enjoyed joking and clowning around, it quickly became common knowledge that he could not take a joke being played on him, which caused him even more problems. Because everyone knew that Deangelo and Buck were best friends, no one messed with Deangelo. He was usually able to avoid altercations. He also enjoyed a small amount of prestige.

Chapter II

Deangelo and Buck were strolling down their usual route to the school bus three blocks away. The driver had arrived early, and students had already begun boarding the parked vehicle. They were carefreely chatting, discussing the coming weekend, and generally "shooting the breeze" as they waited to begin their long trek across town.

They attended City High School and were bussed daily, even though Lincoln High, also in Pasadena, was within walking distance. Many of the kids did not understand why they had to travel so far when there was another school that was closer to them. Few of them knew that this plan had been initiated several years earlier, by the Pasadena Unified School District, in an effort to desegregate the previously predominantly white school.

It appeared to be an average day for the two of them. The summer sun beat down early this particular morning, promising another sweltering day. They were used to dealing with the heat and were dressed in baggy shorts and T-shirts with sandals. It was Friday and they were anxious to get the day over in a hurry because the weekend had finally come.

Buck had big plans and was so excited, his adrenaline steadily rose with the anticipation of the events of the next few days. He had thought long and hard about approaching Deangelo in the past, but somehow now, more than ever, the time seemed right.

He decided he would fill him in on the details Saturday night. Finally, he was going to introduce Deangelo to Speedy, one of the biggest drug dealers in Los Angeles. He was a major distributor and was well connected in the drug world. He was known for squandering plenty of money, having fine women, and driving fancy new cars. He lived in a half-million dollar pad in View Park, a high-class neighborhood in the heart of the city of Los Angeles. He was also known for the extravagant parties he held in his plush, spacious home.

Speedy was going to plug them in and help them come up the ranks.

Buck had been working for him for some time now. Speedy felt he could trust him and began talking to Buck about fronting him some packages of cocaine. He told Buck he would let him pay after he had gotten rid of it. This would give them a chance to make some real money.

He would start by giving Buck an once for five hundred dollars. Buck would be able to pay him back and make one thousand dollars for himself off each sack. Buck could easily turn a package like this at least five times a night. The only reason Speedy had made the offer to Buck was that he was such a fast worker. In Buck's mind, with Deangelo helping him, the possibilities would be endless.

Buck lived alone with his mother and had always come and go as he wanted. The older he became, the more his mother left him alone. She was not as involved as Deangelo's mother, and sometimes he wished they had the same close relationship his friend had with his mother.

*   *   *

That day, Deangelo's main concern was to get back to a Ping-Pong tournament he was winning at the local Boy's Club. He, and everyone else involved, knew that there was no one at the club who could beat him, and he couldn't wait for his moment of glory whey they handed him the trophy, and a check for fifty dollars, for the third year in a row. He had already made plans to buy his mother a gift with the prize money. He was going to get her that nice, new watch she had admired the last time they were at the mall together.

Last month, they had gone shopping for some clothing for Deangelo's nephews, when she noticed the watch in the window. She was drawn to it as they walked past the jewelry shop. She had been needing a new watch for some time now, and this was the first one that had really caught her eye.

They went inside so that she could try it on. It fit her delicate wrist as though it was made just for her. She seemed to glow like the shining gold on the modest timepiece she was wearing, but when the salesman told her it cost fifty-five dollars, she paused. She gave a long sigh as she gazed at the watch one last time.

She then handed it back to him, politely saying, "Thank you sir, but I don't think it's for me."

Deangelo had been planning to surprise her all week. He couldn't wait to see the look on her face when she opened the package. He felt she deserved it and knew she had sacrificed buying it for herself in order to get school clothes for the boys.

Playing Ping-Pong and shooting pool were like second nature to Deangelo. Both games came easily to him and once he started playing, his concentration could not be broken. He spent most of his time on the tables whenever he could.

Playing these games, and being able to go swimming were the main reasons he went to the Boy's Club each day after school. When he was playing, he felt he had real power, and was in control of at least one thing in his life. For once, he was the top man around, almost like the gangsters in the violent world he so frequently fantasized about, where money did not make a difference. In fact, it was the reward, and he was taking his.

That morning, on their way to the bus stop, Deangelo and Buck were laughing and joking with each other as they often did. Suddenly, Buck began to confide in him. He sensed the seriousness in the tone with which Buck had begun to speak.

"Man, I'm getting ready to come up and that's on the real, dude, and I can take you with me. I got a real sweet deal lined up, and I can cut you in on it—that is, if you're game," exclaimed his young friend. Buck continued, saying, "But you gotta have heart, Homie. This ain't for no punk mothafucka!"

"Dude, what you dreamin' about now? You always got some kinda' shit going on in that thick skull of yours," Deangelo remarked as he playfully rubbed the top of Buck's baldhead. "What is it this time, man? You planning another imaginary bank robbery or something? What kinda' shit you got cooked up now, my man." Deangelo laughed as they reached the bus stop.

Buck stopped Deangelo in his tracks in an effort to let him know he wasn't kidding. "I can't tell you now, but it involves big bank partner, big bank, and I know you can handle that, can't you. You're my boy and I'm gonna look out for you, you know that, so chill out. Just trust me, know I wouldn't come at you wit' no bullshit, man."

"What's up?" questioned Deangelo, as he finally began to start grasping the severity of Buck's mood. He couldn't help wondering what kind of opportunity was about to confront him. What did Buck have in mind? Big bank sure sounded good, but what would he have to do to get it?

"I'll let you know about it when the time is right," Buck explained without elaborating. "There's somebody you gotta meet, man—the dude who's gonna plug us both in. You'll see."

When they boarded the bus, Deangelo's curiosity was aroused. They took their usual seats in the back of the bus. The bus was finally full and it was time to take off. The engines roared as the driver shut the doors. Buck said nothing more about his scheme during the entire ride to school.

Deangelo scratched his head and kept looking puzzled.

"Don't stress, Homie. I'll let you know what's up pretty soon. Just be ready," Buck said, trying to reassure his buddy as they got off the bus. The pair headed to their first period English class.

The high school was a huge complex. Its modern buildings were well kept and well equipped. The school offered an excellent education program, and there were plenty of caring, skilled professionals, whose hearts were into their tasks. Many of them were inspirational to their charges.

A river of students flowed through the complex, each eventually reaching their destination and settling. As the pair entered the room and took their seats, Deangelo overheard some of the students discussing an oral presentation project that was due today.

"The speeches! Oh shit! I forgot about the assignment again," Deangelo moaned, slapping himself on the forehead.

He had been up most of the night watching the movie *The King of New York*. Here another gangster tale that had taken his attention away from his assigned schoolwork. Deangelo sank down into his seat and put his head down on his desk as he waited for the teacher to call the first speaker.

"Please don't call me," he silently prayed.

"Susan Johnson," called Mrs. Avery. "Come on up. You have the opportunity of going first."

Deangelo exhaled with relief; he had gotten a brief reprieve. Everyone knew that when Mrs. Avery selected names from her roll book, she would pick a letter and start calling names straight through the alphabet, beginning with whichever letter she chose. She started with the letter J.

"This is great," thought Deangelo to himself. "Maybe this will buy me a little time," he wondered as he realized he would be the last to be called. Maybe he could make up something before Mrs. Avery got on his case, which he knew was coming. She had been on him lately about developing his writing skills and increasing his commitment to his class work, as well as his homework.

Time seemed to creep along as Susan rambled on and on about taking over her father's companies. Her high-pitched, monotone voice was almost hypnotizing. It seemed as though she would never stop screeching, and making those annoying sounds. She went on and on about "Daddy and the Company."

Most of her classmates had tuned her out some time ago. Deangelo felt his eyes getting heavy and his mind drifting....

Suddenly Deangelo heard Mrs. Avery's voice calling his name.

"Deangelo ...."

He couldn't understand what had happened. It wasn't supposed to be his turn yet. Yet, there she was standing, looking straight at him.

"Well, let's go. It's your turn. I know you're prepared. I also know that you didn't come in this room without your assignment again." Mrs. Avery yelled, "I've had it! You march right down to the detention room. I tried to warn you last time, now you will have to suffer the consequences."

As she pointed towards the door, she repeated her order. "Go on." Flicking her fingers on both hands as one would shoo a fly away, she said, "Get out of here."

"I am so upset with you, 'til I could wring your neck, young man," she muttered to herself as she wrote out his detention pass.

"Come on, Mrs. Avery," Deangelo pleaded as she ushered him out of the room. "Give me one more chance, just a little more time."

"Aw man, that's cold, Dude. You shouldn't let that bitch shove you around like that man," Buck hollered out from the second row.

"Excuse me young man?" Mrs. Avery pivoted around on one foot and gave Buck the look—the one most of the students knew meant not to mess with her. "What did you just say?" Mrs. Avery's voice was stone cold.

"You heard me, bitch! You ain't deaf," replied Buck. He went on, "You ain't suppose to be pushing nobody around like that. Who the hell do you think you are, bitch?" Buck blurted out defiantly.

"That's enough of that, sir. Get up! You can go join your buddy in the detention room," Mrs. Avery stood arms akimbo, neck bobbing, with a "Bring-it-on" look in her stance.

"I'll bring it in tomorrow. I promise. Come on man, give me a break," Deangelo begged one last time, trying to break the tension between Mrs. Avery and Buck.

Mrs. Avery ignored Deangelo's plea and stood firm with Buck. She was adamant. No more breaks.

Both boys relented and bee-lined for the detention room.

When they got down the hall from her room, Buck said, "Man! Fuck this shit! We don't need this bull! If I go to detention one more time, they're gonna suspend me man. I ain't going in there.

He paused for a moment, then said, "Let's get the fuck outta here, dude," motioning Deangelo to follow. "I'll tell you all about my plan to come up on the way over to my cousin's house. It's not far from here, and she'll let us hang out.

"Besides, they probably won't even know that we never made it to detention." Buck smirked. "Come on, dude, let's smash outta here!"

Deangelo found himself heading for the exit. Buck began talking about Speedy and his extravagant lifestyle, and how close they had become. He told Deangelo about all the big players' parties he was known for giving, and how he wanted Deangelo to meet Speedy, too.

By the time they had reached their destination, Buck had explained the entire set up to Deangelo, and he agreed to give it a shot.

Once inside, Buck took Deangelo into a bedroom of his cousin's small apartment and showed him a bag of cocaine rocks. This was Deangelo's first time ever seeing the substance. He stared blankly at the odd looking stones. They resembled balls of chalk. After seeing the package in Buck's hand, Deangelo knew he was about to finally be able to make some real money.

They figured they could get rid of about ten sacks a night, if they hustled. They even talked about working twenty-four hours straight. This could mean a lot more than five thousand dollars per night, for each of them.

Deangelo felt a kind of nervous excitement as he calculated his share of the pot. They agreed to meet at the Boy's Club after the Ping-Pong tournament, then leave from there for Speed's place at about 9 p.m.

When Deangelo finally made his way home, Tion called him and related what had happened after Buck and he had skipped school. Mrs. Avery had gone down to the detention room to speak with the boys and discovered they had never arrived. She, in turn, informed the Assistant Principal Mr. Hunter, who immediately gave them both two weeks' suspension.

Luckily, no one had called his home yet, so his mother didn't know.

"Thanks, Tion for the 411."

Deangelo hung up the phone, relieved. He was relieved because he had a big day at the Boy's Club tomorrow, and he knew he would be grounded once she got the news of what happened at school.

Chapter III

"Man, what a match!"
"Did you see Deangelo wear that ball out?"
"You the man, Deangelo!"

Everyone at the Boy's Club was hooting and catcalling about the Ping-Pong tournament Deangelo had just won. So happy he had won, Deangelo flailed his arms about and jumped up and down. The counselors, Mr. Arnold and Mrs. Lee, looked on at him and smiled. Even his opponent Larry conceded graciously and grinned at him good-naturedly.

"It was just a game, Deangelo. You act like you hit the lotto." Larry gave a flick of the wrist at Deangelo's outward display of emotion.

Ignoring him, Deangelo balled his fist and pull his arm down in the "Yes," sign. Facing the onlookers, he threw up the Victory sign with his index and middle fingers.

He was so excited, he could hardly accept his victory trophy. The people at the center only saw him as a young boy excited about winning a ping-pong match.

But they just didn't know. Tonight he would become a man. He felt like he had just stepped on the path to his destiny. He knew that he was on his way to make a deal with one of the biggest dope dealers in the country. This was definitely going to be a night to remember.

All evening, he had held on to his secret like a little boy hiding a bumblebee in his palms. He didn't want anyone else to know, but at the same time he could only get so close to the secret himself. He tried to concentrate on the game and contain his joy.

Just as he accepted his award, his eyes were drawn towards the door. As Buck walked in, the air around his friend even vibrated. All eyes riveted on Buck. He could feel Buck's energy as he entered the room. He sensed that Buck was equally as excited about their meeting with the top man, Mr. Speedy, as he. As their gazes met, they each saw the look of anticipation mirrored in the other's eyes. They nodded.

Deangelo was relieved when he saw Buck was on time.

"Is it nine o'clock already?" he asked, glancing at the clock on the wall. He was just talking to hear himself talk, he was so nervous. He was stunned at how quickly nine o'clock had arrived.

During the second half of the tournament, knowing Buck was in the audience, Deangelo was relentless. He hit the ball back and forth, ka-ping, ka-pong. It moved so fast that his opponent, an older boy named Jerry, would eventually be unable to keep up with him. Absolutely no one could stop him. It was an easy victory and time had passed quickly as he dominated round after round. He had literally slaughtered each opponent. It was hands down, no contest.

He beamed with pride as he thought about what he had planned to do with the prize money of $50. He now had his trophy and money in hand. He was anxious to get started on the real business of the coming evening. If this evening's deal went down as expected, he would be able to do a lot more than just buy a watch for his mother.

Buck and Deangelo slapped each other a couple of high-fives, turned around, then walked out the door. Deangelo ignored the "good-byes" he heard floating on the air behind them. The two boys waltzed with anticipation, they were so elated.

"This fifty is going to look like chump change, when you find out how much we're going to make," Buck said.

Outside, Buck surprised Deangelo when he led him to a gold-toned Lincoln Towne car and opened the door. His eyes widened

"Man, where did you get this car?"

"My cousin, Mooney, rented it for me. I paid him with the money I made working for Speedy."

"We've got to make a good impression," Buck beamed. "We'll be riding in style."

A huge smile flashed across Deangelo's face as he settled into the plush interior of the Towne Car. He could see himself getting used to this kind of lifestyle.

44

When Buck started the engine, the hum was so low, Deangelo could hardly hear it. Buck pulled away from the curb, turned the corner and rolled onto the freeway. After he adjusted the steering wheel and the seats, he began picking up speed.

Deangelo popped in a tape, reclined his seat even farther, and allowed his head to rest against the soft headrest. He closed his eyes, kicked back, and enjoyed the ride. Neither said a single word to each other. The new car cruised across the highway.

"So Buck, man, you think this dude gonna really do this for us, or what?" Deangelo finally spoke up. He popped in another tape playing the sounds of his favorite old school singer, Marvin Gaye. He crooned to the beat of "What's Going on."

"Just trust me, homie. It's on, man!" Buck assured Deangelo. "We comin' up dude." He eased the speedometer down from 95 miles per hour. "You'll see. So, don't even trip. Everything is gonna be straight. All we gotta do is meet the dude and handle our business!""Right. Right! I'm straight, my brother. Now let's handle our business!" Deangelo exclaimed.

He settled back in his seat once again, grooving to the music on the booming system. He loved the music of the 60's almost as much as the gangster movies on which he found himself fixated.

After a while, they made their way across the freeway and headed towards View Park. It was an affluent area of Los Angeles, which featured grand, Spanish style homes surrounded by sculptured gardens and plenty of privacy. It was considered to be an exclusive district. Most of the cars parked in the driveways of several homes were either Rolls Royces or Mercedes Benz.

Deangelo couldn't help wondering what kind of people lived in homes like these and what they did to earn a living that afforded them such a lavish lifestyle.

Buck explained to him that it was a racially mixed community filled with professional people. The majority of the people living there were doctors or high-paid lawyers.

The neighborhood also boasted a few famous actors and musicians. Somehow, the two boys could feel that there was a certain sense of security that appeared to flow throughout the entire area.

From the outside, Speedy's home was impressive. The two boys were overwhelmed as they wound their way up the walk and approached the huge, double doors. Instead of climbing the stairs, they stopped in their tracks and just stood still. For a moment, they were spellbound by the view.

The house was a giant, two-story structure, which sat on top of a hill. They could see the entire Los Angeles Basin from the front-porch. They stood in awe and looked at the lights twinkling all over the city. Suddenly Buck and Deangelo felt special just being there. To them, this was really living. It far exceeded anything found in their part of town.

Deangelo scanned the neighborhood. Every house on the street was perfectly color coordinated. The lawns were well-manicured. Not a single stone was out of place in the rock gardens. The entire area was immaculate and well-lit. Private security cars occasionally patrolled the area.

The double French doors, which served as the entrance to the mansion, had stained glass windows in the upper halves. As they bounded up the stairs to the front door, Deangelo's mind began flashing with thoughts of some day providing this type of domicile for his family.

This was the kind of life he wanted so badly for them. He imagined that his mother would really enjoy a place like this. He thought about how proud she would be if he could give her something like this. He knew in his heart that she really deserved a *home* of this quality. He also wondered what a house like this would cost and just how long it would take to make this kind of cash.

Buck rang the doorbell. A scantily–clad woman, who only wore sexy, revealing, black lingerie, answered the door.

"Hey, baby. Can I help you?" she asked. She batted her eyelashes in an alluring fashion.

"We came to see Speedy," Buck answered sheepishly. He looked away from the woman's large bust line, which seemed to spill out over the teddy.

The woman seemed non-plussed about her dress or lack thereof. "Come on in," she said in a sultry voice. She opened the door wider, ushering them inside.

Deangelo gasped. He had never seen anything like this! The house appeared to stretch out endlessly. Directly ahead, they could see the living room with its plush white carpeting and French Provincial furnishings. To their right, was a double stairway, one leading upstairs, the other, downstairs. To the left, was a hallway that led to a large country kitchen.

They waited in the vestibule while the woman called upstairs for Speedy. After a while, a man, who appeared to be in his forties, made his way down the stairs. He looked surprised to see the two boys standing there. He recognized Buck. He waved his hand halfheartedly in greeting.

"Hey, man, what's up? What are you doing here?" Speedy asked in a gruff voice. "And who's this dude?" He looked directly at Deangelo, then continued. "Do I know him?"

Buck cleared his voice. "He's my partner, Deangelo," Buck's voice trembled, just slightly. "We came to talk to you about that deal you offered me. We wanna make it happen man— Deangelo and me. We ready for you, if you're still game."

"We! Nigga, you must be crazy?" Speedy laughed, but only for a very brief moment, then his whole demeanor changed. He barked angrily, "Listen man, there ain't no deal, not now! Furthermo', don't you ever bring no stranger into my house—my home, again. I don't do business like this—at home, and most definitely not with a stranger. I made that offer to you. Hell, I don't know that nigga!" Speedy pointed his finger at Deangelo. His anger escalated to the point that the veins stood out like ropes in his neck.

Buck tried to appease him.

"Speedy, it's alright man. This is my homie. He's cool."

Deangelo looked over at Buck. Although he didn't know Speedy, he could tell by the snarl on his face and the glare in his eyes that Buck had pissed him off. At the same time, Deangelo had never seen Buck look so terrified.

Buck spoke in a rush and pleaded with Speedy. "He's my ace, you can trust him, man. We do everything together, and we gonna be partners in the deal." Buck sounded so nervous to Deangelo, he thought he would break down and cry. Speedy paused for a moment, but he sensed the tension in Speedy's balled fist.

Before Deangelo knew what was happening, Speedy walked over to Buck and backhanded him across his face. The clap of the blow echoed throughout the entire house. Deangelo stood frozen like an ice sculpture. His palms sweated and he bit his lip to hide his own trembling.

"I said don't you ever bring anyone into my home without asking me first, man!" Speedy yelled as Buck hit the floor.

He then pulled a gun from the drawer of the small table that sat in the entryway, pointing it straight at Deangelo.

"I should shoot this mothafucka right fuckin' now," Speedy said. His voice was surprisingly low, deadly. "I trusted you Buck, and you go and fuck up like this!" Disappointment punctuated his every word.

"Now I want you two assholes to get outta my fuckin' house, before I kill this dude," he said, as he motioned them towards the door. "Out!" He pointed his finger at the foyer.

Deangelo was in shock as he helped his friend up on to his feet.

"Let's get the fuck outta here, man!" he said, with both rage and fear he stared down the barrel of the nine-millimeter Speedy pointed at him. "We don't need this shit. Let's go, man!"

Deangelo felt his life in danger, but at the same time he felt a rage boiling inside him that he'd managed to suppress most of his life. Red lava welled up inside of him as he thought about what had just happened.

As they made their way to the door, Deangelo whispered to Buck, "We can't let this bastard do this to us." His fear evaporated, he was so livid. He continued. "We gotta get this mothafucka, man." A grim, steely determination laced his words.

Buck responded quickly to his bestfriend's foolish idea. "Don't even think about it D." Buck stared intensely into Deangelo's eyes, his own full of fear. "He'd kill us and our families if we tried anything," he said under his breath. "I've seen him do it once. It's like he goes fuckin' crazy when he gets mad. Let's get the fuck outta here now, and I'll talk with him later."

The two of them dashed back to the car.

Fastening his seatbelt, Deangelo snorted through his nose. "This shit ain't cool man, and if my brother were here, he'd smoke this chump without even thinking about it!"

Buck, obviously in a state of shock, was silent.

Deangelo tried to ignore him as he went on. "This ain't the way it goes, Buck! We gotta show that mothafucka we ain't no punks, man! Hell, nobody would have to know it was us." He thought about the way things went down in the gangster movies he knew oh so well.

The boys rode back home in complete silence. This was definitely not what they had anticipated. Deangelo's mind filled with thoughts of revenge. If he was going to get in the game, he knew he had to do something to get even. If he was going to play, he planned to come out on top. He felt that he couldn't just let something like this go. It was all about one's reputation, and if this ever got out, he felt he would not stand a chance to really come up and be respected.

Before Deangelo knew it, he found himself sitting in front of his house. The ride home seemed to take only a few seconds,

"Don't worry, man. I'll take care of everything tomorrow. I'll give you a buzz after I've talked with him," Buck said.

Deangelo climbed out of the car without a word.

Feeling a rush of fury and exhaustion, Deangelo made his way to his bedroom and passed out on his bed. He was glad his mother didn't get up and start chastising him. He hadn't realized how the day had taken its toll on him as he drifted off to sleep. He slept soundly throughout the night and dreamed about how he would handle the situation that had occurred. He saw himself and Buck waiting outside Speedy's house and blasting on him as he climbed into his car.

Chapter IV

Saturday mornings usually found Deangelo in bed, sleeping late. Generally, it was due to staying up all night engrossed in his favorite pastime, watching one of his favorite gangster movies. This morning was no exception, only *this time* the movie had been *real-life drama*. The encounter with Speedy had been pretty intense and left him depleted.

Around 11:30, the lingering aroma of sausage, eggs and coffee wafted on the air and finally brought him to his feet. After dreaming about it, he had no thoughts of the previous night's events. As he rose, he pondered upon his situation. Why did he have such a yearning for retribution? Once again, he recalled what had actually happened the night before.

He decided to not think about it since he remembered that he was supposed to be getting up early. He'd planned to go down to the mall to buy his mother's gift.

Deangelo was hoping that the watch she had admired would still be there. As he staggered sleepily into the bathroom, he felt really good, proud even, about being able to do something special for her. His mother already had his breakfast waiting on the table for him.

"Good morning, Mom," he said, kissing her on the cheek as he entered the quaint kitchen. It really resembled a breakfast nook. There was only room for a table, stove and four chairs. "I'm going down to the mall in a minute. You want anything?"

"No, thanks, baby," she answered, gently patting him on the shoulder. "But, it's sweet of you to offer though." She began sweeping the kitchen.

He chewed his food slowly, savoring the taste of the sausage, grits, and eggs that were set before him. The sun splashed over the red-

and-white-checkered tablecloth, brightening up the room and lifting his mood.

"By the way, we're expecting a call from your brother today," his mother said over her shoulder, as she filled the sink with water and liquid soap. She ducked her hands in the soapsuds and dipped a glass. She added, "He should be calling soon."

"Tell him I said 'hey'."

Drying her hands on her apron, she sat in the chair and faced Deangelo. "Look, why don't you wait a little while before you go, so you can talk to him?"

His mother's forehead furrowed in worry.

Deangelo knew his mother worried about the distant relationship between him and his older and only brother, Ajulius. Still, for Deangelo, it was a very touchy subject.

Not wanting to worry his mother, Deangelo nodded his head "yes." He agreed to wait.

He finished his breakfast in silence, then returned to his room. Just as he sat down on his bed, the telephone rang. He could hear his mother excitedly calling for him. He knew it was Ajulius, whom everyone called "Penthouse," by the excitement he heard in his mother's voice.

"You know I love you, and I've been praying for you every day!" Bernice said, as Deangelo walked towards her.

His sister, Doris, was standing in line, waiting to talk to her brother. She and Ajulius had always been close. After they chatted the allotted time, she said, "Bye, Ajulius. Love ya." Tears glazed her eyes. She handed the phone to Deangelo.

Although Deangelo had major issues dealing with the absence of his only and oldest brother, deep in his heart, he sincerely loved him.

"Hey, L'il Bro."

Just hearing his brother's voice, Deangelo's love showed in his wide beaming grin.

"Hey, Penthouse! What's up?"

"Never mind me, L'il Bro'."

"What up with you?" Penthouse sounded in good spirits.

"Nothin' much, man, just been kickin' it at school." Deangelo knew Penthouse wanted him to stay in school.

"Oh, yeah? Well, that ain't what I heard," Penthouse's voice intoned sarcastically.

"What the fuck you doin' at Speedy's house, L'il nigga? I thought I told you to stay yo' ass outta the fuckin' game, man!" Penthouse had always warned Deangelo about getting caught up at a young age as he had. "What's goin' on wit' you?"

Puzzled, Deangelo turned away from his mother and Doris. He cupped his hand over the phone and whispered, "Damn, Penthouse! Man, how'd you find out about that shit? It just happened last night. What y'all got in the pen— radar?"

"Look D. I told you there ain't shit that goes on out there that don't come through here within the hour," Penthouse remarked. "Now what the hell are you doing out there?"

Deangelo could hear his brother's anger mounting. To appease him, he began explaining how tired he was of not having the luxuries of life, and how he had decided it was time for him to come up in the world. He told him about the deal Buck had offered to cut him in on. He related the entire incident at Speedy's house from the prior night. When he finished running it down, he had Penthouse believing that he had been helping Buck sell cocaine for some time now. Also, he told him that he was already too far in the game and had no plans of quitting now.

Penthouse was silent for a while. Finally, his voice came back on the other end. "I understand, L'il Bro. It's just I wanted a different life for you. But you do seem to know what you're doing."

He cleared his throat.

"If you're going to be involved in the game, I just want to be sure that you're safe."

Penthouse's plan was to hook him up with someone who would look out for him.

"Take down this number," he told Deangelo. He then proceeded to tell him about a friend of his named Pretty Floyd. Penthouse had saved his life once, while they were both in prison, and he knew that Pretty Floyd would do right by his brother. After all, he owed him.

"Now give him a call. He'll plug you in and watch yo' back," Penthouse said reassuringly. "I gotta bounce now, but stay up, baby boy!"

"Yeah, you too. Good lookin' out, man." Deangelo anxiously wrote down Pretty Floyd's number. "Ajulius..." He paused. "Thanks."

"Sho' you right. Peace."

He hung up the telephone.

The receiver had barely hit the cradle before Deangelo grabbed it up to dial Pretty Floyd's number. After a few rings, he answered. Deangelo introduced himself, telling him that his brother had told him to call.

"Yea man, I've heard a lot about you from your brother," Pretty Floyd said. "Peep this. I'm throwing a *Players' Party* tonight. Why don't you swing through—let's say, between 9:30 and 10?"

"That sounds cool," replied Deangelo. "I'm bringing my homie, Buck."

Pretty Floyd questioned, "And who the hell is he?"

"Oh! He's my partna, and we gonna be doing business together."

"Now look here, boy, I'm trustin' you because of your brother," Pretty Floyd said. The tone of his voice became extremely serious. "D, just don't come at me with no bullshit, and you can bring dude."

"I promise," Deangelo answered eagerly. He tried to envision the happenings during tonight's festivities.

"Cool. Then I'll see you brothers later." Pretty Floyd sounded relieved.

"Thanks, man." Deangelo jotted down the address on a piece of brown-paper-bag, and hung up. This time it felt as if it was really going to happen. He was finally going to come up in the game.

He immediately called Buck to share the seemingly good news. He found it difficult to keep from squirming, as he dialed Buck's telephone number with great urgency. The telephone rang and rang, but just as Deangelo decided to hang up, Buck answered.

"Nigga, get yo' ass over here, right now!" Deangelo yelled.

"What's up, man?" Buck questioned.

"Just get over here now, man." Deangelo was adamant.

"Alright, man. I'm on my way."

Almost seconds after hanging up the telephone, Deangelo heard Buck's knock at the door.

"So tell me, what's up, man? What's really going on?" Buck asked for the second time. He scratched his head, looking bewildered. Deangelo beckoned his best friend inside.

When they had entered Deangelo's bedroom, he closed the door behind them.

Suddenly Deangelo blurted out, "Homie! We's in like Flynn!"

"What? Man, just what the hell are you talkin' 'bout?" Buck raised his eyebrow, his curiosity piqued.

"We in, man," Deangelo whispered. "I just finished talking to my brother. He hooked us up big time, dude!"

"You serious, humph?" Buck questioned. His eyes narrowed. "Look man, don't be fuckin' with me now."

Deangelo held his stare and didn't say anything. After a brief moment of silence, the two boys burst out in laughter, slapping each other high five. Deangelo began telling his buddy about the conversation with Penthouse and all about his Pretty Floyd. He told him about the party they had been invited to attend the same night.

"Damn! Man, I took the car back about an hour," groaned Buck.

"It's alright, man. We gonna ride the bus if we have to." Deangelo knitted his eyebrows and spoke in a very determined tone.

The two boys eagerly discussed their plans for the party. After an hour or so of brainstorming and planning, they decided that they would travel via public transportation. Finally, Deangelo asked Buck to go down to the mall with him. When the two youths left the house, they talked more about the kind of deal they were going to try working out with Pretty Floyd, as they strolled to the bus stop.

"We going to a *Players' Party* with no ride and no females." Throwing his hands in the air, he asked Deangelo, "What up with dat?"

"Don't worry bro', we gonna hook it all up at the party." Deangelo sounded more sure than he felt.

"Hey, just as long as we get there." Buck made a circle with his thumb and pointer finger. Both boys grinned as they boarded the city bus, which let them off directly in front of the mall.

Just as they had begun shopping, Deangelo made eye contact with a woman he considered to be one of the finest ladies he had ever seen. He gasped. She was drop-dead gorgeous. It was as if someone had frozen time the instant their eyes locked. Finally, the spell was broken, and they moved. Their heads turned, following each other.

Deangelo tried to sort through his feelings. Whoever she was, she was breathtakingly beautiful. She had long and flowing hair, with eyes that were almost hypnotizing. Her skin, as smooth and blemish-free as that of a baby, was the richest shade of mocha-brown. Her skin even looked so soft to the touch that Deangelo almost wanted to reach out and squeeze her. She held her head high as she sauntered gracefully through the doors, her hips swaying gently from side to side. Her erect carriage made her appear as regal as a queen. Deangelo rushed outside the store where he was browsing, approaching the young lady.

"Excuse me," Deangelo asked, in a voice that seemed to capture the young lady, "can I speak with you for a second?" Deangelo extended his right hand to her.

She turned to him, then paused, reestablishing their intense visual connection. "I already got a man," she responded, checking Deangelo out all the while.

"So, what yo' man gotta do with me?" persisted Deangelo, now with that wide grin plastered on his face that the ladies always seemed to love. As she began laughing with him, making a lasting impression on his heart, Deangelo could tell that his charm was working.

"Bye-Bye," she said, waving good-bye, as she went back to her shopping.

As she gracefully strolled away, Deangelo just stood there watching her. "That lady is gonna be my *wife* one day," he said to himself. Thinking out loud he said, "Yeah, I'm gonna marry her one of these days."

Deangelo walked back into the store where his friend was still trying to cut a deal with the salesman on an outfit he saw, wanted, but couldn't afford—at least not at the price on the label.

"Man, you is crazy!"

Buck responded, laughing, "And you must be dreaming if you think you can get that honey."

"Nigga, gangsters don't dream; they take what they want," Deangelo boasted proudly.

"Yeah, okay man. Whatever," Buck replied sarcastically. "What we come down here fo' anyway?" He frowned.

Deangelo told Buck about his surprise for his mother as they made their way to the watch shop. It was sitting in the window as though it had been waiting for him. He purchased his mother's gift, then the two of them left the mall.

After all, they had to get ready for the big party they were to attend later on that night.

Shortly after, the boys got off the bus and headed for home. Just when they arrived in their neighborhood, they heard the staccato sound of gunshots ringing out, followed by the wail of police sirens. Without having to say a word, they knew what to do.

They ducked down behind a parked car, as they tried to figure out where the shots had come from and what was going on. A couple of dope dealers were shooting it out over their turf.

Someone was hit and several boys were running as the police approached the area. As far as Deangelo was concerned, it was the "same ole same ole; somebody's child lay dead in the street; and somebody else had just gained yet another spot."

The boys watched the commotion for a minute or two, and then when the police arrived, each jogged home to begin preparing for the party. They agreed to leave at about seven o'clock, since they were riding the bus.

After he gave his mother her gift and she opened it, Deangelo could see a sparkle in her eyes. She had been caught completely off guard, which pleased Deangelo. She was even more touched when she recognized that it was the very same one that she had admired the last time she and Deangelo went shopping together for his sister's boys.

"Deangelo, I love you son and I thank you very much. However, you have to tell me one thing?" Bernice gazed at him with great concern in her voice. Deangelo could tell she was hoping that he hadn't stolen the money or the watch.

"What, Ma?" Deangelo asked. The tone of his mother's voice made him uneasy.

"Where did you get the money from to pay for this?" Bernice asked, looking her son square in the eye. She continued. "I sure hope and pray that you're not out there getting into trouble; are you? You know I don't want you getting all mixed up in that dope and junk out there in them streets."

"I know, Ma." Deangelo looked agitated by his mother's comments. "And don't worry, I ain't doing that," he insisted. He went on, telling his mother about the Ping-Pong tournament at the

Boy's Club, then showed her his trophy. She gave him a big hug, squeezing tightly until she was almost cutting off his breath. Finally, she released him and kissed him on the cheek. Next, she slowly waved her hand in the air, displaying the new timepiece on her dainty wrist.

"Thanks, Deangelo."

Deangelo and Buck were both sharply dressed in three-piece suits, silk shirts and ties, with shiny, new patent-leather shoes as they began their long ride across town. They would have to transfer, but only once, in Downtown Los Angeles. They figured the whole trip would take them about two and a half hours at the most. As they got off their first bus at the transfer stop, they noticed a long white stretch limousine with its hood up directly across the street. The driver was trying to get the engine started and was having no luck at all.

Deangelo had an idea. "Sounds like the starter's dragging," he said to Buck, walking toward the driver.

"Got a hammer or a large wrench; or just something I can use to tap the starter?" Deangelo asked, gesturing toward the driver.

The driver nodded, pulling out a small hammer from a tool chest in the trunk. He then handed it to Deangelo, who took off his jacket, attempting to locate the starter. The driver gave him a blanket to lie on so that he did not get his clothes dirty. He gave the starter a few light blows, then instructed the chauffeur to try turning the engine over. The car started right up, purring like a kitten.

The grateful driver offered to take them anywhere they wanted to go in return for their assistance. They told him about the party and he agreed to drop them off, as well as to pick them up, then take them home when the party was over. The boys were elated, for they would arrive at the party in style.

"It's on!" Deangelo exclaimed as he and Buck slapped hands in the air. They scrambled into the back of the limo. They both bubbled with excitement and squirmed in their seats. Deangelo ran his hands across the white leather interior.

"Now this is living," he murmured to himself.

Deangelo could feel his life changing, as he began to assume the gangster role he was about to play. "I can see having all this; real soon," he thought to himself, as he and Buck rode through the city, heading towards the party. A kind of fearless hardness was emerging from him. No one in his family would have believed that they were being chauffeur driven to Hancock Park, in a brand new Lincoln Towne Car Limousine.

Pretty Floyd lived in a multi-million dollar mansion, located in the heart of Hancock Park. All the homes in this area were extravagant. This was truly the lifestyles of the rich, if not so famous. They drove up a large mountainside to a sprawling estate on top. His place looked like a sultan's royal palace. From the driveway, the view of the valley was breathtaking.

From their view in the driveway, Deangelo noticed a massive swimming pool bending around the side of one of the buildings.

The sounds of the party filled the air, as Deangelo and Buck pulled up to the house. People were laughing, dancing, playing cards and dominoes, and gambling. There were expensive Rolls Royces, Benzes and limousines in every direction streaming from the driveway.

It looked as though everyone was thoroughly enjoying himself or herself.

A valet opened the door, directing the boys to a red velvet carpet that meandered its way up to the main entrance of the house. Deangelo got a number from the driver so they could call him when they were ready to leave. They both shook hands with their new friend, then began their journey up the red velvet road.

When they reached the door, a butler in a white tuxedo with tails, answered.

"Pretty Floyd?" Deangelo tilted his head.

The butler bowed. "Welcome." They were invited inside.

There were beautiful women everywhere as the party went on in full swing. Pretty Floyd gave them a warm greeting and made them feel welcomed.

"I've heard lots of good things about you, man," he said to Deangelo, as he began introducing them around. After a while, Pretty Floyd told the boys to go get some food and drink and mingle for a while.

"We'll talk business later," he said, as he left the boys in order to greet some other newly arriving guests. They grabbed a couple of drinks from a passing waiter's tray, then began to explore the party.

A female caught Buck's eye, so Deangelo went on alone. He smiled and shook his head as his friend began to make his play. He watched Buck chat for a while, then wander through the house, guzzling drinks. He became the center of attention among a group of females. Deangelo heard him trying to convince them all to go to the swimming pool with him. He figured Buck was playing since he didn't swim.

Deangelo decided to explore the grounds. The main house was huge, complete with servant's quarters and a bowling alley. People were partying everywhere. Some guests were out on the tennis and basketball courts; others were at the horse stables and riding grounds, while the majority of them filled the enormous rooms of the elegant main house.

After a while, Deangelo wound up in the family room. A group of men were playing dominos and standing on the sidelines betting. He sipped on the same drink the entire evening, watching the game. Finally, he was invited to sit in on the domino game he had been watching. Of course, he could not resist.

Several times Deangelo caught sight of Buck and nodded. They both were having a good time and each had made new friends. This was the first time they had enjoyed themselves for quite some time.

After a couple of hands, Deangelo saw Pretty Floyd signaling for him to come over. Deangelo gestured back, asking for a minute or two. He left the game, found Buck and pried him away from the ladies. They met Pretty Floyd at the entrance to the long hallway. He led them to one of his private rooms in the rear of the house.

"I'm gon' cut to the chase," Pretty Floyd started out. He offered to give them nine ounces up front, giving them a chance to make ten thousand dollars. In a matter of minutes, they wrapped up the details of the agreement and swore a bond for life. They shook hands, then hugged, confirming the set up. Satisfied, they all rejoined the festivities of the party.

Buck, who was now feeling the effects of all the alcohol he had consumed a little more than he realized, went back outside to find that the ladies had decided to get in the pool after all. He pretended he was about to fall into the pool, which had everyone laughing.

Deangelo had started roaming throughout the house, admiring Pretty Floyd's possessions. Everything was decorated in light ivory—the plush carpet, the sectional sofa, even the baby grand piano. He liked his style. He was impressed. Trying to appear older than his fifteen years, Deangelo greeted people along the way as he strolled through the large mansion.

Suddenly, Deangelo looked up and thought he must be seeing things. Was he dreaming? He thought to himself. It looked like the girl from the mall had just walked past the hallway leading to the kitchen. He rushed over to the door and looked in both directions. Suddenly he saw no trace of her. He collected himself momentarily. He wondered if he'd witnessed a mirage and if his mind was playing tricks on him.

"I must be tripping," he muttered to himself. Although he never really stopped looking for her that evening, he didn't see her anymore.

Deangelo began to notice that something was going on outside, so he quickly made his way to the door. He was looking for the girl. But instead, what he saw made him holler.

"Buck!"

He'd walked into the back yard just in time to see Buck laying face down in the pool. The other partygoers were laughing.

Everything happened in a blur after that.

"Look at how long he can hold his breath," Deangelo overheard one person say.

Everyone thought Buck was joking, allowing his body to somehow float motionless in the water. Knowing that Buck could not swim, Deangelo darted towards the water, dove in, then pulled his friend up from the bottom of the pool. He swam with Buck on his back.

"What's going on?" One woman asked frantically.

Another one of the ladies screamed when she finally realized that Buck hadn't been joking this time.

"I think he's unconscious," another lady cried out.

Someone had already called the paramedics by the time he lifted Buck's limp body from the water. Another drug dealer whose name Deangelo didn't know tried to apply CPR. After what seemed like forever, Buck began spitting up water. By the time the paramedics arrived, they only needed to work on Buck for a brief moment before loading him into the ambulance. Deangelo couldn't believe what was happening. A strange feeling came over him, as silent, fearful tears swelled in his eyes.

Several people from the poolside decided to go to the hospital. Deangelo, rode in a limo with a couple of Pretty Floyd's men. No word on Buck's condition had come down yet by the time he entered the waiting room.

Everyone was standing around solemnly conversing, trying to get more information, when suddenly someone yelled, "Fuck Buck! Let's go back to the party y'all!" Everyone looked. It was Lover Boy. He was a lightweight dealer and did not seem to care about what was going on. He did not really care because he did not know either of the boys.

For a moment, Deangelo's mouth flew open in disbelief. How dare this fool act like his friend's life didn't matter. He became so furious, he charged towards Lover Boy. Pretty Floyd's man, Gator, stopped him.

"Be cool, young bro."

He and Deangelo had begun talking back at the party and had been hitting it off quite well. He was the one who had offered to drive Deangelo to the hospital after the accident.

Just then, a doctor entered the waiting room with a blank look on his face.

"I'm sorry...Are there any family members here?"

Deangelo could not hear the rest of what the doctor said. His ears felt stopped up, and he could only see that the doctor's mouth was moving up and down. All he knew was that Buck did not make it. Gator pulled out his cellular-phone, calling Pretty Floyd to inform him of the fatality.

Deangelo's knees buckled. His arms and legs felt too heavy, he was so weak. His tears gushed out, and he was unable to stop them from flowing from his shock-filled eyes.

"He shouldn't have been in there fuckin' around," Lover Boy commented. "Let's get the hell outta here!" He and a few others made their way to the exit.

"I'm gonna kill that nigga, man!" Deangelo promised Gator. He tussled with Gator and tried to get at Lover Boy again. Gator pulled his arms and held him back once more.

"Chill out, man! There's a time and a place for everything," Gator said, gripping Deangelo by his shoulders, in an attempt to calm the young boy down. He went on. "Don't even trip on this shit, it's taken care of." He now hugged Deangelo, trying to ease his pain.

A few minutes later, Pretty Floyd walked in, embracing Deangelo. "You straight, L'il man?" His gold-toothed smile showed a genuine concern for Deangelo. "Everything's gonna be alright. You gotta be tough young bro'. You gotta be tough or the streets will eat your ass up!"

Deangelo decided to go tell Buck's mother in person what had happened.

Chapter V

The next day, Pretty Floyd sent his chauffer to pick up Deangelo. When they arrived back at his house, Pretty Floyd offered his condolences.

Without further adieu, he got down to business. They talked for a minute, then Deangelo left with his nine ounces.

Pretty Floyd sent Gator over to his house to show Deangelo how to prepare his product, and soon, business was booming. Deangelo tried to hide what he was doing from his mother, but she seemed to know.

Deangelo and Gator began spending lots of time together and were becoming close.

Deangelo never knew that Pretty Floyd had assigned Gator the task of looking out for him and watching his back. The two of them hit it off well and their friendship grew at the same pace that their business did—swiftly.

Within the first week, Deangelo turned the stuff over so quickly that the next time Pretty Floyd gave him a whole kilo.

Deangelo had so immersed himself in his business for the first few days after Buck's death that he was able to go through the motions of living. It wasn't that he had forgotten his friend or didn't grieve for him, but the fact that he knew this is what Buck would have wanted—for him to "handle his business."

However, that morning was Buck's funeral, and that was all that he had on his brain. He wasn't doing any business this day, he decided, at least not until the service was over.

Chrysanthemums and orchids filled the church, adding to the mournful atmosphere. The organ music sent chills down Deangelo's spine. Students from their high school and people who had been at the party packed the pews and the balcony. It was as if the mourners were divided into two camps—the working stiffs and the hustlers.

After the soloist sang "His Eye Is On The Sparrow," Buck's mother had to be carried out of the church as she had fainted.

Deangelo had a rough time, too. He had never lost anyone close to him. The loss of his buddy was difficult to accept.

"Why? Why did you have to go and leave me so soon, man," he sobbed, as he dragged himself towards the casket.

"You alright, man?" Gator asked, meeting him at the casket.

"Yeah, man, I'm alright." Deangelo tried to control his tears. He turned his attention back to his best friend, who lay before him in a casket, dead. Death seemed so strange, so incongruent with Buck's young body.

Placing his right hand over Buck's heart, he vowed, "But I'm still gonna get that Lover Boy for disrespectin' you, man." He then stood there, in silence, staring down at Buck's lifeless body, then began drying his tears.

Gator whispered in his ear. "Hey D, you ain't said nothin' but a word. It's already been taken care of. Don't trip on that," he assured him.

In route to the gravesite, the caravan passed Lover Boy's house. Deangelo, noticed the police cars, and the yellow tape surrounding the front of the yard, then saw a dead body on the ground. He glanced over at Gator.

"It's already been taken care of," repeated Gator. He reached over and patted Deangelo's back, trying once again to comfort him. Realizing what had gone down, Deangelo hugged Gator, and vowed they would be friends for life.

"Man, we in this thing for life"

It meant a great deal to him that Gator would do something like that for him. Buck was his closest friend and Gator's avenging his death touched him deeply. The two made a permanent bond.

It was obvious to everyone who knew Deangelo that he was never quite the same after Buck's death. A strange kind of hardened, street sense seemed to come over his thinking, as well as control his actions.

Soon after Buck's death, Deangelo and Gator decided to become partners, agreeing to gather an army of workers. They made plans to contact several guys who were being released from prison. They were going to set them up with clothes, money, and houses, where they would live and sell for the two of them; thereby, hoping to win their loyalty. Before long, their plan was flourishing. They had houses set up throughout the entire city, with a growing legion of soldiers.

Since Deangelo had access to such large quantities of cocaine, most of the local dealers started coming to him. He worked out deals with the majority of them, slowly beginning to take control of their spots. He and Gator decided that they would call their operation "*G. L.*," for *Gangster's Love*. They vowed that whoever was with them was coming up, and whoever was in their way was going down. Deangelo decided, also, that he would start calling himself "D-Money." He liked that very much, it was his gangster name, and it made him feel powerful.

The cash was rolling in fast, and Deangelo had not spent a dime yet. He had found a perfect hiding place in his mother's basement and was putting his cash in shoeboxes, watching them stack up. Only he and his partner, Gator, knew about the stash. He had collected over forty thousand dollars in about two weeks. He hadn't made any plans to spend the money but kept building it up like a stockpile.

Deangelo hadn't given much thought to returning to school, not when he could make money this fast and with such ease. He went a few days a week, for about a month or two after being suspended. Most days, it was to *handle his business*, as he would boldly state.

One day, he was riding the bus home from school, when a couple of his classmates were getting on his case.

"Oh yeah, nigga? Well, if you making so much feddy, then why don't you go buy yourself one of those new Caddies over there," his friend teased, breaking out in hysterical laughter. He pointed towards the local Cadillac dealership as they passed it by.

"Maybe I will. Yeah, I'll do just that!" proclaimed Deangelo, suddenly realizing that he could pay cash for it, if he chose to.

Deangelo talked the bus driver into stopping, letting the boys get off. They all then headed for the dealership. Deangelo began inspecting the spotless new vehicles. Spotting the inquisitive youngsters, one salesman asked, "May I help you gentlemen?"

"Yeah. My homeboy want to buy a new car," chuckled one of the youngsters. "He might want to get one for each of us," he continued, laughing all the while.

"I like this one. How much is it?" asked Deangelo, nonchalantly, sitting behind the wheel of a brand new, blue, ragtop Seville.

"You have good taste," replied the salesman. "That one is about twenty-eight thousand, but we might be able to work a good deal for you." The tone of his voice, as well as his overall demeanor, indicated that he was not taking Deangelo seriously at all.

Deangelo questioned, "How much then, if I pay cash?"

"If you pay me cash, my young friend, then you can walk out the door for twenty thousand;

but you'll need someone of age, with a valid driver's license."

Deangelo's friends were no longer laughing when he called Gator, asking him to go to house to get the cash; asking also for his assistance with the matter of someone with a valid driver's license. Approximately one hour, Deangelo handed the salesman twenty thousand cash, then drove off in his new car. His friends were ecstatic as he drove them each home. His reputation was building and this really earned him the respect of his peers.

Finally heading home, he realized that the he couldn't just pull up in a new Cadillac, without his mother questioning him. What would he tell her? He decided to park the car around the corner from his house until he could figure out what to do. The next morning, Deangelo left the house as though he was catching the bus as usual. He turned the corner, then hopped behind the wheel of the shiny new Cadillac.

Word had gotten around pretty quickly at school, and eventually Doris found out and confronted her brother. He finally showed her the car. She was filled with excitement when he showed her the registration with his name on it. She promised not to tell their mom before he did, as long as he drove her wherever she wanted to go. This arrangement worked well for the two of them, and Doris kept his secret well.

A few weeks later, Deangelo and Gator were cruising around Los Angeles, taking care of some business. Deangelo pulled up to a stoplight, then looked over at the car next to them. It was Speedy glaring over at him, talking to one of his boys. Deangelo could sense that he was talking about him. They each said nothing to the other with their eyes locked, as they drove through the changing light. Deangelo, burned rubber, then proceeded to tell Gator all about what had happened between Speedy, Buck, and himself.

"I'm gonna have to deal with that nigga some day man. I just know it!" said Deangelo, quickly changing the subject.

Gator asked Deangelo to stop by La Rhonda's house, who just happened to be his ex-girlfriend. They had been having major problems lately, and he was planning on moving out. He had promised her earlier that he would come by to bring her some money. Deangelo sat, waiting in the car, when he suddenly heard them yelling at each other. Gator walked out the door, heading towards the car, as La Rhonda ran after him until she was close enough to grab a hold of his arms. He turned, then slapped her across her face, knocking her to the ground. She began screaming wild threats.

"My brother's gonna kill you, man!" La Rhonda screamed as loudly as she possibly could, struggling to lift her fragile body from the ground.

"Man, let's get the fuck outta here," Gator said to Deangelo, who quickly drove away.

"You alright, man?" Deangelo asked.

"It's all good, partna. I ain't trippin," replied Gator.

They decided to give Pretty Floyd a call, to handle some business since they were in the city. He answered, then invited them over. When Deangelo walked in, he was completely taken off guard. The vision of beauty that he had approached in the mall had just opened the door. He was almost speechless as they greeted each other.

"Small world," she said.

"Yeah," Deangelo responded, still in shock. He followed her in disbelief, as she led them to the den.

It turned out that she was Pretty Floyd's daughter and although he had not seen her, she had checked him out several times at her father's place. Her name was Brook, and Deangelo was entranced. Pretty Floyd knew she was interested because she had questioned him about Deangelo several times. He didn't seem to mind since he could see that the feelings were mutual between the two youngsters.

He made it very plain and obvious to Deangelo that his daughter's happiness was his only concern. Deangelo promised to always look out for her best interest and to treat her with the utmost respect. Deangelo invited her to a picnic he was giving the following day, then they exchanged phone numbers. They would grow very close, despite the events of the next few days. He and Gator took care of their business with Pretty Floyd and were on their way.

The boys had been planning the picnic for some time now, and everything was going as planned. Everyone showed up and was having fun. There was plenty of food and drink, and the weather that day was so perfect, that it only added to the success of the gathering. Brook was helping Deangelo host the picnic. Everyone in the family seemed to like her as she was warmly accepted into the clan. Deangelo was especially excited because his mother had agreed to come. He had invited her to Bar-b-ques and picnics in the past, but she would never show.

"I love my son, and I want him to know it!"

"He's gonna be so happy that you're actually coming, Mama," replied Doris. "It means a lot to him."

Deangelo's entire family was at the park, all waiting for Bernice to arrive. Deangelo's face lit up with joy when he finally saw her car turning into the parking lot. His mother, Doris and her boys, got out the car, then eagerly joined them. Bernice greeted everyone, then began serving plates. She enjoyed the company of her relatives and was actually having a good time. Everything seemed perfect as the afternoon grew late. Then out of nowhere, shots rang out, as bullets came raining into the picnic area. Everyone ran for cover, as a car sped past. Deangelo could see that it was La Rhonda's brother, Terrell, and Speedy. They had come after Gator for slapping his sister.

Deangelo looked around frantically to see if everyone was safe. Luckily, it appeared that everyone was okay, when all of a sudden, he noticed a few of his cousins crowded around someone lying on the ground. He ran over to see who'd been hit. It was his mother, she was motionless in a pool of blood. She had been killed instantly, when the two bullets penetrated her chest and head.

"Wake up, Momma! Don't die!"

Deangelo was so outraged, he and Gator jumped into his car, with a few of his boys, speeding off in an attempt to chase down the shooters. The car was nowhere in sight as the boys zoomed up and down street after street.

"Those niggas are fuckin' dead!" yelled Deangelo, unable to hold back his tears. "They fuckin' killed my moms! Those mothafuckas think I'm soft man, but I'll show their punk asses," he cried. Gator eventually convinced Deangelo that it would be better to calm himself down first, then plan out his revenge, rather than racing wildly through the city streets.

When they returned to the park, a large crowd had gathered, and the police were everywhere. They questioned Deangelo for what seemed to be hours, but he said nothing, nor did anyone else. Thoughts of getting even were the only ones that raced through his mind, as he continually refused to comment to the police's line of questioning.

Chapter VI

The day after the picnic, Deangelo, who seemed to have completely metamorphosed into gangsterdom, went on a rampage. From now on he wanted to be known only as *D-Money*, the main "G." He was rolling high and on top. Business was good, and the money was flowing.

His mother's death had freed him into the mobster world, as now he felt no restrictions. She was the only person he respected, the only one who would give him guidelines and would keep him in check; and now, she was gone. Now he was sure he could take that step forward with no fear. He knew he could take over and have no regrets.

The rage and anger inside Deangelo grew with each passing day. It was like a burning inferno, sweltering inside. Pretty Floyd supplied him with an arsenal of weapons, and he and Gator went on a serious mission, looking for Speedy and Terrell. They were relentless and left a trail of death and destruction in their wake. They decided that their adversaries would have to pay with their lives. There was no way D-Money was going to think about letting his mother's death go unavenged.

Her passing was a little more than he was prepared to handle, and in a sense, he had already snapped from the pressure. He had thought about several ways of getting even, slowly torturing the two of them, cutting their heads off in front of their children, or maybe killing their families as he had seen so many times in the violent movies he loved so well. Nevertheless, all he could really think about was getting revenge. He figured that he would probably end up drilling a few bullets through Speedy's and Terrell's hearts. He and Gator went to all of their known spots, terrorizing and kicking in doors.

The first house they came to, they burst in, then, instantaneously, began shooting up the place.

"Where the fuck is Speedy?" yelled Deangelo, firing the guns he was holding in both hands.

In a wild frenzy, they killed everyone in sight, not really giving anyone a chance to respond. "They ain't here, man. Maybe they done already left town," smirked Gator, in a sinister voice, as he looked over the three dead bodies. The two boys gathered up the money and drugs, then moved on.

They had been told that Speedy and Terrell would both be between several places, and they would hit them all if necessary. D-Money was beyond containment as he fired more shells into the corpses asking them of Speedy's whereabouts, as though they could answer.

They weren't quite sure if Speedy and Terrell had been tipped off or not, but it didn't matter. They hit spot after spot, house after house, but for some reason or another, they were never able to catch their elusive enemies. They always seemed to stay one step ahead of D-Money and Gator.

When they reached the third spot, they decided to start offering their victims the opportunity to join them or die. Anyone who hesitated was taken out without a moment's thought. Before it was over, eight people were dead, and their army had grown tremendously. They kept chasing them day after day, until they had hit nine spots. By this time, it was common knowledge that both Speedy and Terrell were on the run. The two were nowhere to be found. Knowing he had completely crippled Speedy's operation, Deangelo was content to wait for a while until they surfaced.

D-Money was becoming increasingly ruthless in his business dealings. He began to pressure people who owed him, and threaten their lives. One of his clients, Busta, was so intimidated that he became desperate and robbed a bank in order to pay his bill with D-Money. Busta had owed D-Money two thousand dollars for some time now and had been avoiding him, when suddenly he looked over and saw him walking towards his car. Busta sat nervously as he approached while he sat at a McDonald's drive-thru-window.

D-Money got out of his car, walked up to his associate's car window leaned in and put the barrel of a thirty-eight in his mouth. "I want my money, man, I don't wanna hav'ta blow the back of your head off," D-Money warned casually.

"Okay, man. I was coming to see you; I just need two days, man. That's all," whimpered Busta. "You don't hav'ta do this. Come on, man, you know me. I'll take care of you," he pleaded, terrified to no end.

Busta let out a sight of relief, as D-Money agreed, and withdrew the gun's barrel from his mouth and walked away. Busta collected his order and drove home trying to figure out where he was going to get the money he had lost gambling. When he got home, he watched an episode of "Starsky & Hutch." He studied the screen intently as he watched how three men laid out their detailed plans, dressed themselves as women, and then robbed a neighborhood bank. Their plan was flawless and they got away, scot-free.

With a glow in his eye, Busta decided that he would do the exact same thing tomorrow at the local bank. D-Money had put such a fear in his heart that he would do just about anything to be able to pay his debt. That was coming way too close to death for his comfort. He convinced a couple of his buddies to join him. They followed the plan to the letter, donned their disguises then headed for the bank. In no time, they found themselves speeding off in the get-away-car. The plan worked so smoothly that they hit the same bank three days in a row.

One of Busta's cronies, Rodney, was prone to seizures, and all three times, he had almost gone into a fit from all the excitement. Nevertheless, both his partners decided to try a fourth time. Busta declined, as he was happy to have paid off D-Money. At the bank, everything was going well for the robbers; they had collected more money this time than all the previous trips combined.

As they ran for the cars, Rodney had an attack, dropping his bag of money beside him. He lay convulsing on the ground, when the police arrived.

*   *   *

Bernice's funeral was the only thing that put a temporary halt to D-Money's rage. Brook went with him and was his only source of comfort. He had guards posted everywhere to ensure that things went as planned. He sat stone-faced as the service went on. He was suffering deeply seeing his mother's body lying before him, but this time, tears wouldn't come. He could only sit there, thinking about finally catching up with Speedy and Terrell.

When he went up for the parting-view of his mother's body, Deangelo walked slowly making his way forward with his arm around his sister, Doris. Suddenly, she screamed, "This is all your fault! You killed our mother!" Crying uncontrollably, pounding on his chest, she went on, "How could you do this?"

All Deangelo could think to do was embrace his sister, but before he could, she slapped his face, screaming, "I hate you! *I HATE YOU!*"

He stood speechless, as his sister's words pierced his heart. After standing there, starring blankly at his sister, he walked over, kissed his mother's corpse, then walked out with Brook and Gator close behind him.

Brook told Gator the directions to their family's beach house. He left D-Money and Brook at the door and drove away. For the first time, Deangelo took his mind from his business and thought of vengeance. He knew that Gator would handle things, so he could give his full attention to this beautiful creature beside him.

Brook did her best to console him. He could not take his eyes off her, as she did her best to make him comfortable. He eventually held her close, kissing her lips gently. She slowly melted as he nibbled on her ear, then began tenderly kissing her neck. The foreplay mounted as they tore each other's clothes from their bodies.

He lavished her body with his mouth and hands as he made his way around her sexy figure, exploring her womanhood. Deangelo felt as though he had stepped into another world as they passionately made love, over and over again. Their bodies churned, as their yearning for each other grew stronger with each embrace. Finally, they lay entangled in the satin sheets that once covered them.

Brook then began questioning Deangelo about his feelings on settling down and starting a family. She told him how she feared for his safety because of the gangster life he was now living. She attempted to talk him into getting out of the game. He kissed her gently, then said, "Maybe, one day; if I had the right reason. Yeah, maybe one day."

They stayed at the beach house for about a week, getting to know each other better and making love. It didn't take Deangelo long to realize he was falling in love.

Chapter VII

Time passed quickly after that week at the beach house. D-Money and Gator spent a few more nights riding around in search of Speedy and Terrell but were never able to catch up with them. After a while, Deangelo began to cool down, his need for blood relinquishing its hold on him. He finally began to focus on other things, mainly his drug empire, and his relationship with Brook. He and Gator looked out for each other as they handled their business.

The organization was steadily growing at an unbelievable rate, as did D-Money's reputation, as word of his dealings circulated. They were selling more and more cocaine, as the epidemic spread deeper and deeper throughout the surrounding communities. He had six houses in five cities now and was always making plans to expand.

The police had been coming around Deangelo's sister's house and a few of his spots asking questions about the murders at Speedy's places. They weren't getting any information, but they were pretty sure that it was D-Money and his men, although, there was no solid proof of the fact. This seemed to really get under the skin of one detective in particular. He swore that he would bring D-Money down, no matter how long it took, or what he had to do to do it.

The boys had been careful, and left no traces of anything that would connect them to the killings. The detective with the bad attitude brought D-Money and Gator down to the station for questioning once, but had to let them go for lack of evidence. He even attempted to set them up a couple of times, but those attempts also failed, as luck appeared to be on Deangelo's side.

Deangelo and Brook spent plenty of time together in the days that followed. Eventually, they decided to move in together. They rented a nice three-bedroom house in Altadena, as their relationship was becoming much more serious. Brook was constantly talking to Deangelo about getting out of the game and letting go of his dope houses. Her main concern was his idea of avenging his mother's death.

"No good can come from it, Baby, and it sure won't bring her back," she would tell him. "Just think about what she would want or what she would say to you. You know she wouldn't want you to go out killing someone else," Brook reasoned. Her words were beginning to hit home.

"You're right, Sweetheart, but this is just something that I gotta do," he replied, stroking her hair, planting loving kisses on her lips.

In his heart, Deangelo knew that Brook was good for him, also, more than ever, he wanted to be with her; but he did not see why he could not have the best of both worlds. With the money he was making, he would easily be able to provide Brook with the kind of lifestyle to which she had become accustomed while living with her father, Pretty Floyd. He imagined everything picture perfect and began thinking about asking her to marry him. He even mentioned it to Gator once.

"You two seem to be good together, and remember, you did say you were going to marry her when you first saw her in the mall," joked Gator. "Seriously though, man, if she makes you happy, then you should go for it bro." The large smile that spread across Deangelo's face signified his agreement with Gator's comments. He said no more about the subject.

A few weeks later, Deangelo and Brook were on their way home from his sister Doris' house. She had apologized to him for her behavior at the funeral and the two of them had been there for each other throughout the whole ordeal. Doris and Brook had become like sisters and were continually begging Deangelo to get out of the game. Brook feared for his life and was afraid of losing him to the streets.

Brook was driving and had stopped at a neighborhood market to pick up some wine and cheese. Deangelo had just begun walking across the parking lot, when a gunshot was fired, the bullet piercing his shoulder. The sound from the gunshots panicked everyone, as people ran, screaming, for shelter. Again, shots rang out, and, yet again, Deangelo was hit. He tried to return fire, but was unable to tell where the shots were coming from.

When the cracking of the weapons finally ceased, he had been hit four times. Once in the leg, and three times in the chest and shoulder. "You can't kill me, you sorry ass! I am gonna live forever! Come on out and fight me like a man, you coward!" He screamed furiously, as blood flowed from his wounds. He fired aimlessly a few times, then collapsed.

Brook was hysterical. "Someone help me!" She screamed bent over him.

The ambulance and police both arrived quickly, and Deangelo was rushed to the hospital. Everyone in the parking lot was questioned, but no one had seen anything. The police got the same story from everyone they asked, they all heard shots, ran for cover, eventually seeing Deangelo take several bullets, then go down. They never found out who fired those shots that day, but Deangelo was sure it was Speedy and Terrell.

For the first time, Deangelo began to have second thoughts about his relationship with Brook. What was he doing to himself? Was he becoming to soft? Had he let his guard down because of her? These questions stayed with him while he rode half-conscious in back of the screaming vehicle. However, his doubts were instantly dispelled when he woke up, finding Brook and Gator by his side.

"I was so worried about you. At first, I thought you were..." she said, choking on the thought of losing him.

"Don't worry, Baby, I'm alright. I'm sorry you had to go through all this. You could have been hurt too, and I wouldn't be able to handle that," Deangelo said, trying his best to comfort her.

"Word on the streets is that it was Speedy and Terrell," said Gator. "I was tracking them down earlier, and now I've got some boys out looking for them.

"Call them in; don't worry about that right now. We'll handle it ourselves when I get outta here," Deangelo quickly responded.

Gator took care of business for him, as usual, and Brook visited every day. He had been lucky; all four bullets missed his vital organs and were lodged in muscle tissue. They were all successfully removed and he was able to recuperate within a few weeks.

On the day he was to be released from the hospital, Brook told him that she had a surprise for him. He anxiously awaited her arrival, as he signed the release forms. She brightened the entire room with her smile, when she entered, tenderly kissing him. "So, what's the big surprise," he asked, with the anticipation of a young child on Christmas Day.

"I wanted to wait until you were better before I told you," Brook said, teasing him playfully.

"Tell me what?" asked Deangelo, almost cutting her off.

"Well, Mr. Deangelo, I'm pregnant. We're going to have a baby!"

His mouth fell open in surprise. "Are you serious?" He questioned.

"Yes. We're going to have a child, you and me, our baby," replied Brook, sounding tense as she tried to gauge his reaction.

"Come here, girl," said Deangelo, pulling her close. "I love you," he said, as he kissed her passionately. "That's the best news I've ever gotten in my life," he said, assuring her that everything was going to be alright and that he was there for her. "I'd been thinking about asking you to marry me, and I guess this isn't exactly how I'd planned to do it, but I think this is the perfect time. Brook, will you be my wife?" He asked kneeling down before her.

"Yes! Oh yes, I will! I love you, too, Baby!" Brook answered through tears of joy.

The first person they shared the news with was Pretty Floyd, who insisted upon having the wedding ceremony at his house. He had already begun looking at Deangelo as a son-in-law and was delighted that they were going to make it official. His little girl's happiness was his only concern, and since he liked Deangelo, it was all the better. He would easily be able to welcome him into the family. They decided that they would have the elaborate affair some time in August. Deangelo's brother, Penthouse, would be coming home in July, and the baby was not due until March.

Since Brook had agreed to marry him, Deangelo decided that he was going to get out of the game, in order to be with his family. He and Brook had talked about developing some land in Colorado that he had inherited from his grandmother. They also decided that they were going to build their dream home there one day. Deangelo planned to begin the building of the house, and then surprise Brook. He thought of giving it to her as a wedding present, but the developers said they needed more time.

He thought it would be perfect for when the baby was born. He was going to pick Brook and the baby up from the hospital, fly them to their new home, and then tell Brook that he was officially out of the game and that, now, he was all hers. Before it was completed, Deangelo would have spent well over two million dollars making sure that everything was exactly as Brook wanted it to be. She had designed the place herself and had shared her sketches with him at the beach house one evening.

Only Gator knew about his plans. He helped Deangelo keep the secret from his fiancée for the months that followed. Brook knew that something was going on, but she had no idea what it was.

Chapter VIII

Deangelo loved Brook and had decided with no regrets to leave the game but wasn't sure just how he would do it. First he began gradually closing down a few of his dope houses, then began opening legitimate business. He acquired a restaurant, a couple of record-shops, a beauty salon, and a Bar-b-que shack. They all did well, making money instantly, most of which, he put into his out-of-state construction project.

He had been closely monitoring the progress and everything was going well. Once

Brook almost found out, when the contractor left a message for Deangelo. He eventually convinced her that it was an out-of-state business that he was thinking about buying. He finally got her to stop questioning him. She decided to trust his better judgment, and gave it no further thought.

The house was going to be beautiful, and he could not wait to see the look on his future wife's face when he carried her across the threshold. He could hardly contain himself. He hadn't felt this way, since he had surprised his mother with her new watch. It felt good, and he knew that he would really enjoy doing things for Brook. He realized that he could be truly happy with her and planned to be a devoted husband and father. He promised himself that he would be there for his children and would not take them through what he had gone through with his father. He was going to spend plenty of quality time with his family and let them know how much he loved them.

* * *

Brook had been preparing for the big wedding, which was now only a month away. She had mailed the invitations, chosen her color-scheme, found the perfect dress, and ordered the cake. Pretty Floyd was having the entire house done over for the ceremony. Rehearsals had begun, and she was in complete bliss as the countdown to her big day narrowed. She was pleased with Deangelo when he began closing his houses. She believed in him and was sure that he would give the game up completely. She also believed that they would share a great future together, if he wasn't killed first. She often wondered whether he would get out in time. She did her best to support his new ventures, hoping her support would help him make his transition sooner.

Brook had begun taking Deangelo to church, and they were getting premarital counseling from the minister. He had warned Deangelo that he would not live very long, if he continued down the path that he was traveling. Deangelo faithfully attended all the sessions, but did not let on that he had already made the decision to change his life.

The day had finally arrived for Penthouse to come home. He had to stay three weeks past his release date, which was how long it took him to lose twenty-five pounds. He had gotten so big in prison that they considered him a menace to society and made him lose weight. Deangelo and Gator were waiting for Penthouse, when the doors opened and he stepped out into freedom. His massive body was like a fine sculpture, almost every muscle rippled with each move he made. He walked right up to Deangelo, rather menacingly, giving him a big hug.

"What's up, man? It's so good to see ya', bro," Penthouse said, his attention turning to Gator.

"And who's this dude? He questioned Deangelo, pointing directly at Gator.

Deangelo introduced his partner to his brother, then they made their way to the car.

"We've got a big party planned for you tonight," Deangelo informed his brother.

"That sounds cool man. Let's party!"

When the *man of the hour* arrived at the party, which was in full swing, he entered the room, shouting, "Hey now! It's been a long time," as he snapped his fingers and laughing as he began dancing about. Deangelo went all out for the party. He and Gator dug up some of Penthouse's old friends and made sure that everything was nice.

While passing each other in the long hallway that led to one of the guest-restrooms, Deangelo asked Penthouse what kind of car he wanted. His older brother looked at him in disbelief and said, "It really don't matter, man. I mean, anything is fine, as long as it runs."

What Penthouse was not aware of was that his younger brother had already purchased a used Mercedes for him.

Doris was glad to see her brother, although at first, she was a bit uneasy around him. There was a certain wildness in him that frightened her. They laughed, joked and danced the night away. Deangelo showered his brother with all kinds of gifts, clothing, and personal items that he needed.

The party went on until early the next morning. Finally, but slowly, the guests started leaving, and it was obvious, that, all the festivities had worn Penthouse out.

He had decided to leave with a former girlfriend, and everyone else went home. Before he could leave, Deangelo handed him the keys to the Mercedes, but Penthouse just stood there, seemingly in shock. The look in his eyes, as they rapidly darted between the car and Deangelo revealed just how pleasantly surprised he was.

The next day, Penthouse went to Pretty Floyd to ask if he would set him up with a package. Pretty Floyd listened to his proposal, but finally told him to talk to his brother. For some reason, which Pretty Floyd couldn't understand, this seemed to anger him a little. Although Deangelo had provided his brother with everything he wanted, Penthouse couldn't see himself going to him for his help. He felt that it was something he had to do on his own. After all, he was the older brother, and it was he who had given Deangelo the connection in the first place.

"You owe me, man," he insisted.

"I paid my debt when I set your brother straight!" snapped Pretty Floyd.

"It was what you wanted, and Deangelo turned out to be a good investment, and I thank you for that."

"Peep game Penthouse. I like the way he does business," Pretty Floyd explained, "I know that I can trust him. He's already proven his loyalty. Together, Deangelo and I that is, we have everything down to a science. Things are going great, and to be honest with you bro, I ain't going to change that for anyone," explained Pretty Floyd, his patience growing short.

"Hell, he's my main man, and that's who you will have to deal with, too. Now quit trippin' and go talk to your own brother." Pretty Floyd could see that Penthouse wasn't too pleased or happy with his response, but they were friends, and ultimately their meeting ended without incident.

Penthouse had made several connections, while he was locked up, and he decided to make use of them. He made a few contacts, and soon, had arrangements to buy a large package. He had set the deal up with a friend, and the two of them were supposed to meet some guys in about two hours. They would have to travel to Inglewood to make the transaction, but it would be worth it.

Things appeared to go smoothly, the deal went down exactly as planned. However, when Penthouse got home with his product, he discovered that the quality was nowhere near what it should have been. He wasn't going to be able to make close to what he had expected. The guys had obviously tried to beat him, so he immediately got on the telephone and began complaining. They told him not to worry and to just bring the package back, and they would take care of things.

Not much went on in the world of dope deals that didn't reach Deangelo. He had gotten wind of the shady deal Penthouse had made about an hour before he was supposed to return his package. Deangelo discussed the problem with Gator, then tried to talk to his brother.

At first, Penthouse denied everything. "What you talkin' 'bout? Man everything is cool, and it ain't nothin' I can't take care of."

"Why didn't you just come to me man? You know that I've got everything that you need, and that you don't have to deal with nobody else," said Deangelo, a little agitated with his brother.

"Truth?" Penthouse questioned, then paused for a second. "Okay then, here's the real, man. You've done enough already dude and this I can handle myself. I just wanted to make a little cash, so I could pay you back for some of the shit you did for me."

"You don't owe me nothing man! You're the one who hooked me up with Pretty Floyd, and that I haven't forgotten. All of those things that I did for you, was my way of trying to pay you back and to say thanks," explained Deangelo. The two of them talked for a while, then Deangelo tried to get him to let he and Gator go along with him, but Penthouse insisted that it was his problem and that he had to be the one to handle things.

Once again, Deangelo felt the space that had always been between them as kids. He just couldn't get through to his older and only brother, which bothered him a great deal. Penthouse was his blood; moreover, he loved him very much. They were getting nowhere, so

Deangelo decided that he and Gator would follow Penthouse just to be on the safe side.

"Those are some scandalous niggas, man!" He said to Gator, as they tailed Penthouse, who was unaware of their presence. "Ain't no telling what them punks might try."

Deangelo and Gator pulled up minutes after Penthouse and his buddy entered the dope house. The three guys inside took the package back, telling Penthouse to relax for a minute. Deangelo got out of his car just in time to see someone sneaking around the side of the house. He was holding a gun, trying very carefully not to be seen.

Deangelo quietly crept up behind him, just as he was about to enter the front door. He placed the cold barrel of his gun against the back of the would-be-sniper's head while Gator went around back.

Deangelo yelled for his brother as he walked the captive inside. Seeing what was going on, Penthouse was relieved to see his younger brother was watching his back.

"You bastards tried to set me up," he screamed, then went berserk, shooting everyone in sight, being careful as not to hit Deangelo or

Gator. After the three guys inside the house were down, Deangelo pulled the trigger of his gun, then watched as the fourth man's body hit the floor. They jumped into their cars, speeding off long before the police could or would arrive.

Once they returned home, Penthouse hugged his brother, as he thanked him for saving his life. Deangelo was hurt because Penthouse hadn't come to him in the first place. Later, he told Penthouse and Gator that he wanted to turn the business over to them one day and wanted to know if they could work as partners.

Deangelo loved Gator like a brother, and it was important to him that they would be able to get along. Penthouse looked over at Gator then hugged him. The three of them shook hands in agreement, officially welcoming Penthouse into *G.L.*

They decided to discuss the details later. Deangelo knew that he could trust Gator, but he had serious questions about his brother. He pondered over his thoughts, wondering if his brother was going to keep up his end of the deal. He remembered how volatile he could be and how sporadically he changed his mind. He could be pretty headstrong sometimes and wasn't always willing to take advice. Gator was smart and a brilliant businessman.

Deangelo respected his opinions valued his advise. He needed to know that things would be okay between him and Penthouse if he were to make them partners. He set Penthouse up with a package, and then he and Gator gave him control of three of their main houses.

Chapter IX

In the days that followed Penthouse's initiation, Deangelo and Penthouse didn't see very much of each other, except for an occasional Sunday dinner at their sister's house. One Sunday, they had been together most of the day; and after everyone had finished dinner, Penthouse began asking questions about his mother's death. This was a subject that had been previously avoided by each of them.

All Penthouse knew about it was that his mother had been hit by a stray bullet, while picnicking at the park. When he heard the details about Speedy and Terrell from his sister, Doris, he became enraged, blaming Deangelo for their loss. His yelling caused the boys to begin crying.

Doris sent them next door to the neighbor's house. Just as the boys left the yard, Penthouse yelled, "You didn't even get the mothafuckas, you little bitch!"

He then charged his brother, then hammering his powerful fists into Deangelo's broad chest.

Deangelo did his best to reason with his brother, but it was to no avail. He did everything he could to defend himself but was no match for his muscular sibling. They destroyed most of the living room as they tussled. They broke lamps and turned tables into toothpicks. Doris became hysterical, as she tried breaking her brothers apart. She tried stepping between them, as she had seen Bernice do in the past. In his rage, Penthouse hit her with the back of his arm, as he drew his massive fist back to punch Deangelo again.

Doris screamed as she went flying across a table, landing on the floor. At the very same moment, a large painting of Bernice fell from the wall and shattered. Seeing this, without warning an awesome silence swept over Penthouse, which suddenly stopped his assault on his younger brother. He gazed around the room, as though he was in shock. Bernice had been the only person able to bring him out of his wild rages, and she had succeeded again. He began picking up the broken fragments of the keepsake and tried to piece them together as though they were a puzzle. Frustrated and unable to make the pieces fit, he began to cry.

Doris and Deangelo shared his pain as they looked on in amazement. He fell to his knees sobbing profusely. This was the first time they had ever seen him in tears. Then, strangely enough, they too began to weep.

They both embraced Penthouse and all three of them shed tears for their mother, as they bonded like never before. They each felt closer than ever as they tried to comfort the other. The moment of closeness, Penthouse pushed away from the two of them, jumped to his feet, then ran out the front door without another word.

The next day he called Doris and persuaded her to make a conference call to Deangelo. Penthouse apologized to them both.

"We are family, and we've gotta stick together," he told them. "Besides, y'all know Mama would want that."

They all agreed, then began discussing the repairs to Doris' house and a few personal family matters, then began making plans for dinner the following Sunday.

August was approaching fast. In less than a week the wedding day would finally arrive. Pretty Floyd's mansion was immaculate; everything was perfectly coordinated in Brook's favorite colors; peach and gray.

Deangelo could not choose between Gator and Penthouse to be his best man, so he asked them both. The wedding party was beautiful, and Brook was breathtaking in her gown. She wore a long, sleek gown with tiny pearl buttons down the back.

The sun shone brightly and it was a gorgeous day. The ceremony began on time and went smoothly, as planned.

They shared special vows they had written. Brook pledged her undying love and devotion. Deangelo had everyone in tears as he professed his love in return. He promised to do whatever necessary to protect, provide, and care for her. Brook knew in her heart that it was his way of telling her he was giving up the drug business, which added to her bliss. She had no idea when, but she knew he would do it eventually. She melted as he lifted her veil, then kissed her passionately. They had finally become husband and wife.

Pretty Floyd was strutting around like a proud peacock. Although there was a complete staff of helpers and servers, he saw to it personally that everyone was comfortable. His little girl had become a woman, and now, she was married.

Deangelo had become a genuine member of the family which pleased Pretty Floyd very much. Brook was happier than he had ever seen her; this made him ecstatic. He had to fight back the tears when he walked her down the aisle. Later he surprised them both when he gave them a trip around the world as a honeymoon present.

"The gifts are all so lovely. Thank you so much." Brook beamed at her father, as they looked over the two huge tables piled high with beautifully wrapped packages.

As the happy couple posed for the photographer, Deangelo thought if only his mother could have been there, sharing this special moment and milestone in his life, how proud she would be. He was saddened by the thought that she would not be around to witness the changes he had finally made in his life.

Nevertheless, he sensed her presence strongly, as Doris whispered in his ear, "You know, Mom's somewhere watching," with tears filling her eyes, for she, too, was ever so proud of her little brother. She continued, looking Deangelo directly in his eyes, "I know she's happy for you, as well as proud." Then she hugged him tightly, holding him in her arms for a moment, just as their mother would have done.

Fighting his own tears, Deangelo replied, "I love you, sis." He kissed her on the cheek.

They danced all night, as the two families got to know each other better. To everyone's surprise, Penthouse was unusually happy. He was boasting about his little brother and how happy he was going to be with his new wife. When it came his turn to dance with the bride, he pinned ten one-hundred-dollar-bills to her gown. Later, he slipped ten more bills in his brother's pocket.

"Just some spending change, bro'," he said, as they embraced.

The entire day was like a dream come true, everything went exactly as planned, and the affair was a huge success. Everyone who attended the wedding, talked about what a lovely couple they made, and how beautiful the ceremony had been. Everyone, also, told them that they were made for each other, as they wished them health, prosperity, happiness, and a long life together. Deangelo and Brook started their trip early the next morning.

Penthouse and Gator had become pretty close, and business was going well, as usual. Gator seemed to understand Penthouse and gave him his space. There had been several murders in the area, and rumors were circulating that Penthouse was responsible for them. The police had questioned him a few times, but he always had an airtight alibi. Gator knew in his heart that Penthouse was the culprit, but he never said anything about his suspicions.

He was becoming concerned that Penthouse might cause the police to start digging deeper into their operation. He had decided that he would talk it over with D-Money when he returned home.

Because of his notorious reputation, Penthouse had not had any trouble collecting his debts. However, one day he had gone to a local park and was relaxing with his lady-friend. After a while, he noticed one of his workers, Ace, standing under a tree. Ace was supposed to have paid him for a package the week before. Penthouse made his way over to Ace and asked for his money.

Penthouse could be very intimidating. The frightened dealer began explaining that he was not able to move the package fast enough and that he needed a little more time.

"I tried calling you, man, but I couldn't catch up with you."

Penthouse grabbed him by his collar; pulled him close, demanding that he give him whatever cash he had on him. He then began shaking him like a rag doll.

Ace was a muscular lad, about six-feet-two-inches tall, and weighed about one hundred ninety pounds. Nevertheless, Penthouse jerked him about as though he weighed one ounce. Terrified at what Penthouse might do to him, he nervously began turning his pockets inside out, in an attempt to prove he had no money. Penthouse finally let him go, saying, "Alright man, you got 'til tomorrow," releasing his grip on the frightened young man. "Please don't make me have to come looking for you."

Ace had been selling at the park before Penthouse arrived and had given his money to one of his partners, when he saw him drive up. He had stuck his drugs in his underwear. "Don't make me have to hurt you boy," Penthouse warned.

"I ain't crazy, man, and you know I wouldn't lie to you," replied Ace.

Just then, one of Ace's customers whom he had supplied earlier, approached him with another sale. Hearing this, Penthouse ran towards him like a speeding locomotive, knocking him to the ground on impact. He snatched him up onto his feet, then pinned him against a nearby tree. Ace's buddies watched in terror but dared not interfere. They all knew that Penthouse might kill them for just being there.

After slapping Ace around a few times, Penthouse reached down into Ace's underwear and pulled out the plastic bag filled with rocks of cocaine. Penthouse landed a fierce blow to the abdomen, followed by a right cross, which broke Ace's jaw.

"I want the rest of my fuckin' money tomorrow punk!" Penthouse demanded, then returned to his girlfriend, as though nothing had happened.

Chapter X

Gator and Penthouse were moving large quantities of various drugs at an unbelievable rate. Things were going exceptionally well for G.L. Every one involved was driving new cars, and money problems were a thing of the past. Pretty Floyd had an endless supply of cocaine direct from Columbia. His organization was high tech and ran smoothly. He had the West Coast sewed up and was responsible for the majority of the drugs supplied to the United States.

All of the new businesses that Deangelo and Gator had acquired were prospering, with a couple of expansions as well. The Bar-b-que shack and the beauty salon needed more space to accommodate the demands of their clientele. Business was really booming at these sites. Doris was running the salon and was open seven days a week. She needed more space to hire more stylists to keep up with the steady flow of customers. This would mean that she could close the salon on Sundays and Mondays.

Everyone in town was going crazy over the Bar-b-que. Deangelo and Gator both knew from the beginning that they would have to get a bigger shop or open other locations when they took over the rib joint. Deangelo had used a recipe for sauce which was passed down in his family for generations. It was a huge success and the rage for the ribs was rampant.

Gator found a mini-mall with several available units. It was a great location, with plenty of parking and would be perfect for both businesses. He was negotiating the purchase of the entire complex. He thought about opening other stores in the rest of the vacancies. The owner had not considered selling the complex, however, he was intrigued by the cash offer Gator put on the table. He had flat out refused to sell, until Gator showed him a certified check. They agreed to meet again when Deangelo returned from his honeymoon. Gator felt confident the deal would go through and knew that Deangelo and Brook would be happy.

The police had raided a couple of G.L.'s houses but were never able to catch them with anything significant enough to hold any of its members. Rather, they broke into the house, then proceeded to arrest everyone inside. The occupants all lay face down on the ground as the cops loaded them into the squad cars. They were all at the station only a few hours, and then right back in business that same evening. They were able to dispose of the drugs before the police entered. The officials knew they would not be able to hold them when they took them down.

According to one of the higher-ranking officers, it was to send a message. That message being, they were determined to bring G.L. down. Several houses had been under surveillance for some time now, and the police were constantly looking for more incriminating evidence.

A few days after one raid, the police returned to the same house. This time, they found a couple of guns hidden in the garage. It was one of the rock houses Penthouse was running. When they came in, he just happened to be there. Luckily, he had come by to tell his workers that their package would be delayed and was not carrying any weight as usual. The police arrested, then interrogated him for hours about the guns and the recent murders in the area.

Penthouse was becoming agitated by the repeated drilling. As usual, they got nothing from him. The guns were legally registered to one of the men living in the house. The ballistics tests proved that they had not been used recently, making it impossible to link them to any recent killings. The police had no other choice than to release him from their custody. They even went as far as to try violating him, but, luckily for him, his prints weren't on any of the weapons, and they were not able to connect him with the guns or the murders, in any way.

He insisted that he was not aware that the guns were there, "I don't live there, man! I was just kickin' it with my buddy. How am I supposed to know what other folk got hidden in their garages?" He protested angrily, trying his best to control his temper.

Gator was keeping tabs on the progress of the million-dollar dream home Deangelo was having built for his new bride. Everything was going according to schedule. The land was cleared, and the structure was almost complete. In fact, the contractors thought the house might be ready at least a month ahead of the projected date. Gator knew that his partner was anxious to spring his surprise on Brook and could not wait to tell Deangelo the good news. He was glad he had something positive to report because he was not really sure as to how Deangelo would react to the conversation about Penthouse. Nonetheless, the killings continued and the police were growing more and more suspicious of Penthouse. They were getting closer to the G.L. than they had ever been before.

Time seemed to fly as the money pilled higher and higher. Gator was handling the purchase of a local dry cleaners for Deangelo and had made a better deal than they had anticipated. As always, it appeared they could do no wrong, no matter what type of business they were investing in. By the time Deangelo returned G.L. Cleaners would be in full operation.

Although both Gator and Penthouse had been on constant lookout, there still had been no sign of Speedy or Terrell. Word on the streets was that they had left town and had contracted a hit on D-Money. Penthouse had caught wind of this while gambling one night. A group of the fellas, who were unaware that Penthouse was D-Money's older brother were talking. One of the boys turned out to be Terrell's brother, Bernard.

He was bragging about how his brother was going to bring D-Money and G.L. down the same way that they had done his business. "Yeah, man, when they catch up with them dudes, it's gonna be curtains," he boasted. D-Money was going to pay with his life, and anyone who got in the way would be taken out as well.

Penthouse said nothing, continuing with his card game. Finally, Bernard and his homies left. Penthouse threw in his hand, then followed them.

Bernard was driving alone, so Penthouse asked him for a lift. Bernard opened the door and let him in the car. They talked about gambling for a while, then rode for a minute or two in silence.

"So, you're Terrell's brother?" Penthouse questioned, finally breaking the silence.

"Yeah, man. You know him?" Bernard asked.

"Yeah! We go way back, where is that dude anyway?"

"Why you wanna know?" Bernard quickly questioned Penthouse.

"Because, you bitch-ass-nigga, I'm D-Money's brother," answered Penthouse, as he stuck a revolver in his side, instructing him to drive to an abandoned warehouse.

Perspiration began to pour from all parts of Bernard's body as he drove.

When they reached their destination, Penthouse ordered him out of the car, then fired a right cross to the center of his face. He hit him so hard, you could hear his bones crack.

Penthouse drug his limp body inside then tied him up with an extension-cord he had found. He wrapped some of the cord around Bernard's feet, then hung him upside down from the rafters.

The building had been abandoned for years, and no one ever came there. Bernard hung there, bleeding, for about ten minutes. When he became conscious, he opened his eyes to find Penthouse standing in front of him. As soon as he was able to clearly focus his vision, Penthouse kicked him in the head. He swung from side to side, like a tetherball, as he cried out from the excruciating pain that ran through his body.

Penthouse stuffed an old rag in his mouth, and you could not hear a sound that Bernard was making. "Now, I am gonna ask you this one last time," roared Penthouse. "Where the hell is Speedy and Terrell?" He pulled the rag out of the dazed boy's mouth.

"I told you, man! I don't fuckin' know!" Bernard answered, both frustrated and afraid for his life. "He didn't tell me where he would be, man, honest. I don't know," he insisted, "I don't know, man. You gotta believe me."

"Wrong answer," barked Penthouse, as he hit Bernard so hard that he almost brought down the beam he was hanging from. Blood began to run like a river from his head as he returned to unconsciousness. "This shit ain't getting me nowhere," Penthouse thought to himself. He began to walk towards the exit, then turned laughing, as he emptied his gun into Bernard's suspended body. He wiped the gun and Bernard's car clean of his fingerprints, disposed of the weapon, then walked to a phone to call Gator for a ride home.

Along the way, Penthouse told Gator all about Bernard, except for where he had left the body hanging.

"It's cool, man, we'll catch those niggas," said Gator. However, he could not help thinking, that if Penthouse had not been so eager to kill, they might have gotten more information from Bernard. He didn't say this to Penthouse however, because he hadn't been there and wasn't exactly sure how things had gone down. He thought about how D-Money had gone wild when they first set out after their enemies, realizing just how much alike his partner and

Penthouse could be at times. After all, they were brothers.

A few days passed, and it was now the day before Deangelo and Brook were supposed to return from their honeymoon. Gator and Penthouse had gone to Pretty Floyd's house to handle some business. Pretty Floyd told them that he had spoken with his daughter and D-Money while they were in Rome. They were having the time of their lives and would be home tomorrow. Brook had shipped several gifts, mementoes, and souvenirs from the world tour home to her father's house. There was a package for both Gator and Penthouse. The three of them admired their gifts as they spoke about their business. Finally, Gator and Penthouse completed their transaction then left.

They went to Penthouse's spot, where they began preparing their product for distribution. Penthouse had a few drinks, made a few phone calls, then prepared to leave. They began delivering packages to their houses. Just as they were about to leave the last of their places, they saw a black Mercedes pull up in front of the house and stop.

Gator had noticed the car earlier. He thought for a second that it seemed to be following them but hadn't given it any real consideration nor did it become a major concern because he hadn't seen them again until now. Suddenly, at the same moment that Penthouse stepped onto the sidewalk, the passenger jumped out of the Mercedes.

"This is for Ace, from Speedy and Terrell," he screamed, as he pulled out a nine-millimeter, opening fire on Penthouse.

Bullets went sizzling through the air, seemingly coming from all directions. Gator ducked behind a tree. Two bullets hit Penthouse in the chest, which only seemed to enrage him more as he ran towards his assailant. The hit-man fired two more shots into his massive body, but not before Penthouse, grabbed him, slamming him up against a parked car. Penthouse hammered several bone crushing blows to the hit man's body. Four bullets had gone straight through Penthouse and it didn't seemed to phase him one bit. His strength was unbelievable.

Gator, in the meantime, sent two shots whizzing into the head of the armed driver, killing him instantly. He then turned his attention to Penthouse, who had a death grip around the throat of the shooter. You could see the terror in the choking man's eyes, as he emptied his gun into Penthouse, at close range. Each bullet seemed to give Penthouse more strength as his opponent fired. Gator took aim, then shot the man in Penthouse's grip, blowing the back of his head off.

Penthouse continued strangling the lifeless body of his assailant, even though he, himself, had taken two more bullets in the face. He was like a man possessed as he threw the body of his attacker to the side. Moments later, he turned, taking a few steps in Gator's direction. He just stood straight up for a few minutes, as if he were paralyzed or in shock. Suddenly, he crashed to the ground, landing atop of the dead assassin. Gator ran to his aide, but it was too late.

"Take care of my little brother man," he said. He then drew his last breath.

"No man! Don't fuckin' die! Please don't die on me, bro," Gator pleaded, hugging Penthouse's motionless body.

Gator was unable to stop the tears from flowing. How was he going to explain this to D-Money? He remembered, only too well, how difficult his mother's death had been for D-Money. He dreaded the thought of having to share this kind of news.

Chapter XI

Gator and Pretty Floyd stood waiting at the airport gate when Deangelo and Brook arrived. They had agreed to be together when they broke the news to Deangelo about Penthouse. They both loved him and wanted to do all they could to ease his pain. Pretty Floyd was also concerned about what this might do to their marriage.

He knew all about how Brook had been trying to persuade Deangelo to leave the life of violence, in which he had become so deeply embedded. He wasn't at all sure as to how he would react to his brother's death. He was hoping this wouldn't push him over the edge. He loved Deangelo as if he were of his own blood and planned to support whatever decision he made, as long as his little girl was happy and safe. They had decided not to call him for fear of ruining their honeymoon. He and Gator both felt that it would be better to wait until they were back home, then tell him face to face.

The newlyweds were glowing when they stepped off the huge aircraft. They had traveled around the world for the past several months, and the trip seemed to have been good for them. They looked as if they had been happily married for years.

Looking on, Gator thought about how they were really good for each other. Deangelo looked more peaceful and relaxed than Gator had ever saw him previously.

He so dreaded the thought of what he was about to tell his best friend. He wished for some way to avoid the inevitable but knew what he had to do.

Brook had begun wearing maternity clothing and was looking very much like an expectant mother. Her due date was only a month away, and she was ready. She had a couple of false labor pains when they were in

London and thought for a moment that the baby was going to arrive early. She and Deangelo were out dining when the pains hit her. Deangelo rushed her to a local hospital, demanding the best doctor available.

At first, they thought they might have to cut the trip short, but the doctors reassured then that everything was okay. For the first time, they took pictures of the baby and found out that it was a boy. They were both excited but had already decided that it didn't matter to them either way. Brook was pleased because she knew Deangelo, like most fathers, was secretly hoping for a son.

The doctors assured the young couple that these false pains were sometimes a normal part of being pregnant and that everything was fine. They recommended that Brook stay off her feet for a while and suggested that since they were on a pleasure trip, there was no reason to go back home. They felt it would be better for her to remain and relax.

Deangelo began pampering her even more than before. He watched over her everywhere they went. A few times, he even carried her from the bedroom to the kitchen of their honeymoon suite.

Despite the close call, she and Deangelo had had a great time but were more than glad to be back home again. They all embraced as they met in the crowded airport's lobby.

"Thank you so much, Daddy. Everything was beautiful," Brook said, kissing him lovingly on the cheek. "I had the time of my life, and my husband was wonderful. He's so sensitive, thoughtful, and caring," she boasted.

When Deangelo hugged Gator, he noticed a certain look of sadness in his eyes. He didn't seem to be his usual cheerful self. Deangelo said nothing but sensed that something was wrong.

"So, how's everything going?" he asked turning to Gator as he entered his father-in-law's waiting limo.

"Well, business is great; I have a lot to fill you in on," Gator said reluctantly. "G.L. Cleaners is now open and doing quite well." He dropped his voice. "The houses are cool and that special out-of-town project is almost complete"

"That's great news," replied Deangelo with a huge smile. "So then, tell me, why are you so

gloomy man? You and La Rhonda at it again?"
He chuckled.

"No man, that's all good. We're working
things out," Gator paused for a moment, looking
down at the floor. He cleared his throat and
continued. "But I have some bad news."

"What is it, man?" Deangelo sounded
impatient.

"It's your brother, Penthouse."

"What's he done now? Did he get locked up
again?"

"No, man...he's dead." Gator dropped his
head.

"What?" Deangelo snapped. He was
in shock.

"It was an out-of-town hit," added Pretty
Floyd. "However, Gator and Penthouse took
them out though. It was Speedy and Terrell's
doing."

Gator told Deangelo how Penthouse had
killed Terrell's brother, Bernard.

"This shit is getting out of hand. We gotta
do somethin man," he said, as he explained the
events to his partner.

A hush came over everyone in the car as
Deangelo absorbed what he was being told. The

silence was piercing as Brook tried to console Deangelo. They all waited to see what his reaction would be.

"How?" was all that Deangelo could manage to say.

Gator told him all about the black Mercedes and the hit that was supposed to be out on him as well. He also told him how bravely Penthouse had fought.

"I tried to cover him, but it all happened so fast. I felt so helpless. Man, he saved my life, taking those bullets, and I'll never forget that," Gator promised, fighting back his tears.

Deangelo took his brother's death pretty hard, but didn't blame Gator. He trusted him completely, and knew he had done all he could to protect Penthouse. To everyone's surprise, Deangelo decided not to go on the killing spree that they all thought he would.

"The money ain't worth it, when I'm losing everyone close to me," he said solemnly as he caressed Brook.

His brother's death seemed to further reinforce his decision to leave the game.

For the first time, since the incident with Buck and Speedy, he felt no need for revenge. It all seemed so senseless.

"Where does it all end?" he asked, thinking about his mother and brother and how they died. If only he could turn back the hands of time, he'd surely do things differently.

Being married and starting a family made him understand how precious life truly was. He also realized that he wanted no parts of the endless killing. Somehow, the gangster world was losing its appeal to him. What was the point? It just didn't seem to be right for him to continue the vendetta any longer. He knew in his heart, that this was not what he wanted. Thoughts of retaliation surfaced, but never consumed him.

During his trip, he had promised Brook that even if he didn't leave the drug business, he would never take another man's life again. Unless, of course, it was in self-defense. She meant too much to him, and he would never consider breaking his promise to her. He realized that he loved her deeply and did not ever want to place her in jeopardy again, especially now that they were going to have his baby soon. He just couldn't imagine losing them, no matter what the cost. Nothing would be worth that.

Brook knew that this was a difficult time for Deangelo, so she didn't pressure him. She knew that this would prove whether or not he would truly be able to change his lifestyle. She hadn't wanted to put him to this kind of test, but their future together was at stake. She made up her mind that she would stand by his side, regardless of how he handled the situation. She felt more in love than ever before, when he confided in her that he was not going to go after Speedy or Terrell.

Chapter XII

The funeral for Penthouse was short and private, with only family and a few friends attending. Deangelo was holding up pretty well, although the whole affair served to bring back memories of his mother's burial. He was being torn apart inside, but showed no signs of it on the exterior.

Gator had men posted everywhere, just in case Speedy and Terrell tried anything. If they dared to show their faces, or send anyone, again they would be ready.

Although nothing occurred, as they left the church for the gravesite, Brook was right by

Deangelo's side. As usual, she was a constant source of comfort and support.

Everything was going according to plan, when suddenly on the way to the gravesite, Brook yelled out, grabbing Deangelo's arm tightly. "I think it's time, honey." She grimaced in pain.

He looked at her puzzled for a brief second, then realized she was talking about the baby.

"Man, head for the hospital. Brook's in labor," Deangelo told Gator, who was driving.

Without hesitation, Gator broke the funeral train, racing towards the hospital's emergency room.

"Are you alright, baby?" Deangelo asked Brook, as she moaned louder in an effort to contain her discomfort.

"I'm okay," she responded, gripping his arm tighter.

Deangelo almost panicked, but he wanted to be reassuring.

"Hold on, baby! We're almost there!" He lovingly kissed her forehead.

Deangelo phoned in to the hospital ahead of time, and several nurses were waiting with a wheelchair when Gator pulled up to the admitting door. They swiftly whisked Brook away to the labor room to begin prepping her. She was definitely in labor but was dilating slowly.

Six hours had passed when the doctor came out and informed Deangelo that it would be some time before the baby came. He asked Gator to stay at the hospital while he went home for a minute.

"You sure you don't want me to go for you?"

Deangelo shook his head. "Naw. I'll do it."

The new house was finally completed, and he had taken a picture of it to show Brook when the baby was born. He planned on taking her directly there from the hospital. Just the day before, he told Pretty Floyd all about the big surprise. Everything was ready. Brook's father had taken care of having most of their belongings shipped to their new home. He'd hired a butler, maid, and nurse so that Brook wouldn't have to lift a finger until she was ready.

Deangelo had put aside a couple of bottles of expensive champagne for the occasion and wanted to go buy some roses for his wife. The doctor assured him that he should have plenty of time to make it home and back before the delivery.

"You sure you don't want me to go for you?" Gator asked.

"No, man, it would mean a lot to me if you would stay here." Deangelo headed for the exit door.

On the way home, he stopped at a flower shop, where he purchased a bouquet of one hundred long-stemmed-roses. He was beaming with pride when he told the saleswoman that they were for his wife, who was having a baby at this very moment. She congratulated him and wished them a healthy baby and a long life together. He thanked her and headed for home.

Deangelo had just stepped onto his front porch, when his cellular phone rang. It was Gator.

"Man, if you want to see the birth of your first son, you better get back here. The Doc says it's almost time."

"Thanks, man," Deangelo said. "I'll be back in a flash. I just stopped by the crib."

He hung up, walked into the kitchen, grabbed the bottles of wine, and then headed for the bedroom.

Just as he passed through the kitchen door, gun shots rang out.

Speedy stood in the room, pointing a nine-millimeter in Deangelo's direction. Deangelo had been hit twice in the shoulder. He returned fire, as he fell from the force of the shots. He caught Speedy directly in the forehead, killing him instantly.

As Speedy fell, Terrell came out of the bathroom, unloading a round into Deangelo at point-blank-range. Deangelo was somehow able to return a round in Terrell's direction. One bullet went straight through his heart and he fell backwards to his death.

Deangelo staggered for a second, then fell into a pool of his own blood. He began coughing and spitting up blood. Collapsing, he took his last breath.

* * *

Brooks screams could be heard throughout all the hospital. It was almost as though she was aware of what was happening to her man.

At the same moment, back at the hospital, Brook, who had finally reach ten centimeters, screamed, as the excruciating pain of childbirth got the best of her. "I can see the head, we're almost there Brook," said Dr. Anderson.

Just as the doctor smacked the baby boy's behind, he took his first breath and began wailing.

"Deangelo! Deangelo!" A perspiration-soaked Brook cried out, searching the room for her husband. "Where's Deangelo?"

She could hardly see her newborn son through her veil of tears.

"Deangelo! Deangelo!" Brook let out a soul-wrenching cry which could be heard resounding throughout the hospital corridors.

"Deangelo! Deangelo, wake up!"

This time it wasn't Brook calling him. Deangelo lifted his head and looked around. He had a strange look on his face. Where was he?

Who was calling him? It was his teacher Mrs. Avery trying to wake him. Bored by his classmate's presentation and exhausted from being up all night, Deangelo had fallen asleep at his desk.

Deangelo snapped his head up in shock. Right away, he began checking his body for bullet holes.

"Your report is going to be due tomorrow. No more chances, young man." Mrs. Avery folded her arms across her chest like she did whenever she was serious.

His classmates laughed as he moved about frantically inspecting his body. Sweat was pouring from his face. Suddenly, he broke into a smile with relief. He wasn't dead! He was still alive!

He looked to the back of the room and saw his friend Buck. Buck was still alive! He'd never been so happy to see his friend in his life.

Boy, life tasted so sweet. He never wanted to see another gangster movie in his life, let alone try to be one.

He stood at his seat speechless as he reflected on his recent mental excursion. Finally, he took his seat.

"Mrs. Avery," he promised, "I'll be ready with that assignment tomorrow. Trust me."

He realized that it had all been just a dream. A crazy, crazy Gangster Dream!

Order Form

Milligan Books
1425 West Manchester, Suite B,
Los Angeles, California 90047
(323) 750-3592

Mail Check or Money Order to:
Milligan Books

Name _____ Date _____

Address _____

City_____ State _____ Zip Code_____

Day telephone _____

Evening telephone_____

Book title _____

Number of books ordered ___ Total cost .... $ _____

Sales Taxes (CA Add 8%) .... $ _____

Shipping & Handling $4.50per book.................... _____

Total Amount Due..$ _____

• Check   • Money Order   Other Cards _____

• Visa   • Master Card   Expiration Date _____

Credit Card No. _____

Driver's License No. _____

Signature _____   _____

                                    Date